THE BLOOD WILL TELL

THE LARAMIE HARPER CHRONICLES

J.C. KEOUGH

Copyright © 2020 by J.C. Keough

All rights reserved.

Cover Design: Elizabeth at Elizabeth Mackey Graphics

Editor: Pat Dobie at Lucid Edit

This book is a work of fiction. The characters, incidents, and dialogue are drawn from the author's imagination. They are not meant to be construed as real. Any resemblance to actual events or persons, living or dead, is coincidental, or fictionalized.

No part of this book may be reproduced in any form or by any electronic or mechanical means, including information storage and retrieval systems, without written permission from the author, except for the use of brief quotations in a book review.

ISBN: 978-1-8381373-3-5 (Paperback edition)

ISBN: 978-1-8381373-2-8 (Ebook edition)

For rights enquiries, please email: Jamie@JCKeough.com

For The Night Club VIP Members. You are the best friends, readers, and cheerleaders that any girl could ever ask for. A special thank you to Denyse Sarmiento for trekking the Camino with me and encouraging this crazy writing dream right from the beginning.

ACKNOWLEDGMENTS

When I published *Dying in Dallas*, I had so many wonderful emails, messages, and comments. They buoyed me through the editing and publishing process of *The Blood Will Tell*. Thank you to everyone who reached out to me either directly or by leaving reviews. I'm not going to name you, but you know who you are.

The book is dedicated to the VIP members of The Night Club, but I'd like to take a moment to name them: Deborah Joseph, Denyse Sarmiento, Christina Smith, Beth Sundquist, Catherine Teahan, and Lynne Williams. Your support and shenanigans in the messenger chat keep me writing and entertained.

Pat Dobie, of Lucid Edit, thank you for going above and beyond in your role as editor. You are always willing to be a sounding board and take on the massive job of cleaning up and shaping my stories. And thank you for never yelling at me about my continued confusion over suspension points and non-breaking spaces. LucidEdit.com

CONTENTS

Prologue: Something Wicked This Way Comes	1
1. Mistress of the Night	3
2. Oh, Baby!	9
3. Oh, What a Tangled Web We Weave	14
4. It's Party Time	17
5. A Serpent in the Garden	24
6. The Buckster	27
7. Party Crashers	30
8. One Big Happy Family	35
9. Oh, Baby! Part 2	41
10. Strangers in the Night	47
11. Let's Dance	50
12. Resisting Temptation	56
13. The Chase	61
14. The Platform of Death	65
15. Bad to the Bone	71
16. Trust Issues	76
17. Mind Games	82
18. The Siren's Song	86
19. Betrayed	92
20. Dead to Me	100
21. Gone	106
Epilogue: Something Wicked That Way Goes	108
Enjoyed the Story?	111
Also by J.C. Keough	113
About the Author	115
Author's Note	117

PROLOGUE: SOMETHING WICKED THIS WAY COMES

All Hallows' Eve
Dallas, Texas

The old Victorian house was as gussied up for Halloween as a young girl going to her first dance. Music drifted into the night whenever its front door opened for guests or trick-or-treaters, and light glittered through its downstairs windows. A slight wind had picked up, and the flames in the jack-o'-lanterns that lined the front walk and the wraparound porch danced to its tune. A wooden sign, with 'The Whine Barrel' written on it in dark cursive, swayed over the gate. But the flickering candlelight emitting from the gruesomely carved pumpkins and the dim glow of the waning moon were no match for a dark October night. Inky pools of blackness covered the yard and encroached on the house.

"I can't get over how beautiful it is," she breathed, gazing at the turret that rose majestically for three stories. She and her companion had been watching the house for an hour, taking care to conceal themselves in a long shadow cast by a neighbor's house.

"Laramie always did go all out on Halloween. At least that

hasn't changed," he responded, unable to keep the wistfulness out of his voice.

People had been streaming into the house for an hour, some in costumes, some without. The Halloween party was the perfect cover for their mission. But she didn't completely trust her companion. He was easily distracted in the best of circumstances, and even more so when it came to Laramie.

"Go in, get it, and get out," she said, pretending she hadn't heard his wistful tone. "Nobody recognizes you and nobody gets hurt. Promise me, no games."

"I promise, darling." He reached out to play with a lock of hair that had escaped her cape's hood. Her pretense hadn't fooled him. "No one will recognize me in this getup. It's a straight shot through the house to the cellar, and as long as they haven't moved things around down there, I know exactly where I left it. You keep an eye on things out here. Only come in if I'm in there too long."

"What if she shows up?"

"You are such a worrier. We lost her in Waco. There's no way she could have followed us here."

"We've thought that before. But what if she has?"

"Stop her," he said, his voice hard. "If you can't stop her, follow her in, and don't let her hurt anyone. Get out as quick as possible and we'll meet up at the safe house."

"Okay." She hoped it wouldn't come to that.

"It'll be fine, sweetheart, I promise." He kissed her on the lips. Then, with a quick last kiss on her forehead, he stepped from the pool of darkness and strode toward the house.

1

MISTRESS OF THE NIGHT

**Earlier That Evening
The Madam**

I opened my front door, my fangs fully displayed and bright red blood streaking my lips and chin, clutching a black cauldron in front of me.

"Oh honey, isn't that . . ." Owen waved at my costume. ". . . a little on the nose?" He dug through the contents of the cauldron and pulled out a giant Tootsie Roll, then walked past me into the house. "Not to mention mixing your metaphors, or fairy tales, or whatever."

"Nargh." I removed the plastic dollar store vampire teeth, taking care not to smear the liberally applied fake blood. "It's called irony, and what about you? Cultural appropriation much?"

Owen was dressed as a leprechaun, no doubt to get our friend Grace O'Malley fired up about how the world viewed the Irish. I glanced out the door to make sure the jack-o'-lanterns on the porch were still lit, then leaned farther out to check the sidewalk for trick-or-treaters. There was nary a ghost, goblin, or princess in sight. Fake blood forgotten, I chewed my lip as I turned to face Owen. I'd spent a fair amount of time and money dressing up the old Victorian mansion I affectionately call The Madam to create a suitably spooky yet welcoming atmosphere for Halloween.

"Don't worry, they will come," he said soothingly. Owen is my web designer, dog sitter, new best friend, and, as of tomorrow, roommate at The Madam, the large Victorian house I inherited from my late husband's Aunt Hattie.

"I hope so." I kept my tone unconcerned, but I could tell that I hadn't fooled Owen. Several weeks ago, a community activist had been murdered in The Madam. The police arrested me for the crime. Even though I'd proven my innocence, I doubted that any self-respecting parent would let their child trick-or-treat at a house where a murder had so recently occurred without a powerful incentive. So I'd made it known in the neighborhood that wine would flow freely for the adults who stopped by. Based on the lack of children, I might have overestimated the draw of free booze.

With a last worried glance at the sidewalk, I began closing the door. There was a harsh yip and Dixie, Owen's dog, squeezed through the gap and dove under the skirt of my black Mistress of the Night dress, attacking my bare ankles. I swore soundly and danced back from her snapping jaws. It was more likely that Dixie the rat dog would break a tooth on my ankle than she would break my skin, but it was the principle of the matter.

Bo, short for Bodacious, woofed happily in response. She abandoned her self-appointed guard duties, watching the platters of food on the bar, to welcome Dixie into our home. Bo is a rescue and a mix of several breeds of dog, but the largest part of that mix is pit bull. Her muscular frame makes her look like Goliath to Dixie's teacup rat terrier's ten-pound physique. But like David, Dixie never backs down from a larger opponent. She launched herself at Bo.

"Man, they have a good time together," Owen said, watching them chase each other around the tables in the saloon.

"Not in the house!" I yelled at the dogs. When I realized that I had channeled my mama when she yelled at Monty, Cheyenne, and me back when we were kids, I slammed my mouth shut so hard I might have chipped a tooth. If I had still been human.

I should probably explain. Actually, I should start by introducing myself. Hey y'all, I'm Laramie Harper and I'm a vampire. I'm sure that sounds very 'whatever your addiction is Anonymous,' but I'm new to this vampire thing and a little shaky on the exact protocol for announcing my status to the world. Except . . . I'm not allowed to. It's supposed to be a secret. Whoops. I should probably add that I'm a little tipsy. The night I changed into a vampire, in a regrettable incident I drank the blood of the love of my life. In the two weeks since, I've abstained from blood and have slaked my thirst with wine instead.

We'll circle back around to my killing my true love later. Oh, don't worry, his daddy and our friends resuscitated him, but things have been a little tense between us since. Now, back to the vampire thing. I'm still learning the ins and outs of it, and the wine helps. In an ideal situation, when a vampire is created—a process called The Change—their maker sticks around to show them the ropes. But after my husband Jad Thompson—or ex-husband, as soon as I figure out a way to divorce someone who is legally dead—after Jad changed me into a vampire, he did a runner. His second runner in our relationship. His first one had been two years before, when he'd faked his death to cover up going through The Change himself. He'd let us all believe he was dead for two years, when in fact he'd been skulking around as a vampire. If you can count vampires as being alive. But I digress.

"Earth to Laramie," Owen said. "How about a glass of wine?"

We were still standing just inside The Madam's front door in the large open area that we affectionately called the saloon because of the long mahogany bar that stretched along the rear wall.

"Sorry," I said, "I was just thinking back on the last two weeks."

"Crazy times." Owen had been there for the worst of it and needed no explanations.

"So, are Marek and Grace going to be here tonight?" he asked as we walked to the bar. I refilled my glass with a robust Texas Syrah. Owen selected a bottle from several resting in an ice-filled bucket. It was a crisp pinot grigio, the grapes grown and bottled in a lovely vineyard in the Texas Hill Country. Just as I was about to comment on his good taste, he took several candy corns from a dish on the bar and tossed them into his glass. I gaped at him in horror. He wiggled his eyebrows at me and took a swig of wine.

"Grace said they would be," I said, deciding not to give him the satisfaction of commenting on his candy and wine combination. Odds were he had done it to get my goat, the way he knew dressing as a leprechaun would rile Grace. It was all in good fun, right? "Marek got back from South America about an hour ago, and Grace said they wanted to talk to me after the party. There's something they need to update me on."

Grace O'Malley and Marek Cerny are two several centuries-old vampires who got sucked into my crazy world a few weeks ago, when werewolves attacked me and left me for dead. Jad saved my life by making me a vampire. Oh, don't go giving him credit for saving me. The weres attacked me because of Jad, and he only saved me so he wouldn't feel guilty about it.

Marek and Grace live nearby at the Dragonfly Hotel, which is the crown jewel of Cerny Enterprises, the company they run together. The Dragonfly and The Madam are in an area just north of downtown Dallas, Texas. I'd renovated the first floor of the house to change it into a dog-friendly wine bar named The Whine Barrel. My original plan had been to turn the second-floor bedrooms into a bed-and-breakfast. But since the Dragonfly is also dog friendly, Marek and Grace suggested that The Madam's extra rooms be converted into a dog spa: less work, more money. They are consummate professionals. They haven't found time to teach me much about being a vampire, but we already have business contracts in place.

What worried me is that when Grace said they needed to talk to me about something, she sounded all cloak and daggers. I sensed that tonight's discussion was going to be more about vampires than business.

"What about Van?" Owen asked.

"I hope so," I replied, a tingle zipping through me at the thought of seeing Van. We had talked by phone, but I hadn't seen him in person since the day after The Change. Again, no explanation was needed. Owen knew how much I wanted Van to come to the party, but he was also aware of how tense things had been between us since I had changed into a vampire and killed him. Yes, Van—Van Helsing Anderson, to be precise—was the love of my life, and had finally told me he loved me too, just moments before I latched onto a vein and drained him.

"The Cabernet Cavalry rides again!" Owen said gaily. When I didn't respond, he set his wineglass on the bar. Uh, oh. That meant he needed both hands for the conversation, which didn't bode well. Owen gets animated when he's serious. "So if we get Van and Marek and Grace all here together, we can put a plan in place to search for the True Cross."

"I guess." I stared at the tips of my shoes, refusing to meet his eyes. Owen had dubbed our small group the Cabernet Cavalry when we had unwittingly been forced to take on a vampire crime lord the weekend Jad changed me. But that wasn't why I wouldn't look at him. It was because I didn't want to have the conversation he was clearly determined to have.

2

OH, BABY!

"Laramie, we are going to look for the True Cross, aren't we? It's the only thing that will turn you back to human. If we don't find it, you'll be stuck as a vampire for eternity."

"I can't think about that tonight," I replied. "All I can focus on right now is showing the neighborhood that The Madam, and therefore, The Whine Barrel, is safe." I also planned to show Van that I was safe. That I could be around humans, mainly him, without wanting to drain them. A party was the perfect opportunity to do both. I wanted—no, I *needed*—this Halloween shindig to go off without a hitch.

"Laramie, this is bigger than one night." When I looked up at him, he added, "Not that you aren't rocking the whole Mistress of the Night thing, but what is it you truly want?"

"I don't know."

"You don't know about the True Cross, or you don't know about the vampire thing?"

I shrugged. Honestly, I didn't know how I felt about either. The True Cross was a powerful relic with the mojo to change me back into a human. It could also cure any illness or injury, which made it a valuable asset to whoever possessed it. But it had been missing for decades. Grace and Marek had warned us if we found the True Cross and it fell into the wrong hands, it would cause untold misery to the world. Factions would fight for it over its healing powers. They felt strongly that it should stay lost. But Van hated that I was a vampire and wanted to search for the True Cross to "cure" me. That was why tonight was so important. Showing Van that I could handle the vampire thing would buy me some time to figure out what I wanted. Because let me tell you, being a vampire isn't all bad.

"So, what do you think about the décor?" I turned from Owen and swept my arm around the saloon, trying to change the subject. It was a large open room, all decked out for Halloween. Two small sunrooms opened off one side, while on the other side was the grand staircase, bathrooms tucked underneath. Buckets filled with bottles of wine lined the bar and tables laden with party trays, cookies, and candy were set up near the door to the kitchen. Small pumpkins with tea lights glittering inside them filled the windowsills, and fake cobwebs hung from the large windows. The Madam, and all the time and money I'd spent renovating to turn her into The Whine Barrel, had consumed me for the last year. I loved every inch of her and I loved the life I had created here. Yes, the vampire thing was huge, but I couldn't switch my focus as quickly as everyone wanted me to.

"Honey," Owen said firmly. Realizing my ploy hadn't worked, and that I was about to get what for, I turned back to him and took a huge gulp of wine. A sympathetic "Oh, honey," meant that he was on my side, while a firm standalone "Honey," meant that I was about to get a lecture. "You've really grown in the last few weeks. I've seen you become more confident in your dealings with friends and your family. But you still aren't asking the hard questions of yourself or others."

"But—"

He bulldozed right through. "Questions like, 'When are

we going to hunt down the True Cross?' or 'Van, do you still want to be with me even though I am a vampire?' or 'Do I really want to be a vampire forever?'"

"None of those things are really up to me, are they?" I was starting to resent that Owen would push me like this on such a big night.

His gaze was direct. "Laramie, quit being the victim. This is your life, maybe for eternity. You need to figure out what you want and make it happen."

I stared up at him. The garish orange fake hair that hung from beneath his leprechaun costume's green top hat had turned reddish. In fact, all of Owen was looking a little more pink than usual. That happens now when I get mad: I literally see red. I've gotten better at controlling it over the last couple of weeks, but I'm nowhere near full control.

It wasn't Owen I was upset with. I was angry at myself. Everything he'd said was spot on. But, hey, after a huge, life-changing event a girl needs a little time to adjust, right?

Owen stood watching me, his arms crossed. He knew that I was seeing red, but he trusted me not to go all fangs out and rip his head off. That helped me calm down. Really, Owen made me a better person, or vampire, or whatever. I wanted to say thank you, but a loud pounding on The Madam's back door prevented me. And by loud, I mean thunderous.

Bo barked happily, raced through the swinging door to the kitchen, and headed for the rear of the house with Dixie hot on her trail. Bo loved company and considered herself to be the welcoming committee. Owen and I exchanged a worried look and hurried after the dogs. In anticipation of tonight's festivities, I had locked Bo's dog flap on the back door to prevent her escaping and terrorizing trick-or-treaters. She is a love bug, but unfortunately, cuddles and rubbies aren't what people think about when they see her seventy-pound pit bull self running pell-mell at them. She couldn't get through her locked dog door, but she would throw herself against the flap several times trying.

I put on a burst of vampire speed that almost took the swinging door off the hinges and reached the back door a bare second behind Bo, grabbing her collar before she hit the doggie flap. Dixie launched herself at my bare hand, either because she thought I was going to hurt her friend or because she just couldn't pass up the opportunity. She bounced off my unyielding skin and thudded to the ground. The evil little rat sprang to her feet and snarled at me, showing every one of her teeth.

"Owen, get your damned hellhound under control," I said when he arrived a moment later, panting. "Sit." I ordered Bo. She dropped her back end to about an inch above the floor but continued to wiggle happily.

With Bo and the situation as firmly in hand as I could hope for, I opened the back door. A disheveled woman carrying a large overnight bag pushed past me into the house, pulling two small boys inside with her. She heaved the door shut and leaned against it.

"Bo!" The two boys shouted in unison and fell on my dog.

"Daisy?" I asked, shocked to see my brother Monty's estranged wife in my house. Gone was the petite, perfectly put-together woman who had abandoned Monty last spring to move back to her hometown in Montana, taking their twin sons with her. Her usually immaculately dyed and highlighted blond hair hung in dull, greasy strands, displaying at least four inches of brown roots. While she had lived with my brother in Faith, Texas, Daisy's purchases had practically won our local Mary Kay rep Leena's pink Cadillac for her single-handedly. Now she stood in front of me without a smidgeon of mascara or a touch of lip gloss. But bad hair and no makeup were minor changes compared to the fact that little bitty Daisy, who'd left my brother seven months ago, looked nine months pregnant!

"Wow, Daisy! Monty didn't tell us you're pregnant."

Owen sighed. Proper etiquette says that you're never, ever supposed to refer to a woman's pregnant state unless you see the baby's head crowning. But the shock of Daisy and her ginormous belly in my house had the words screeching out of me before I engaged my brain.

"Boys, y'all take Bo and that . . . dog?" Daisy looked from Dixie to me questioningly and I nodded, " . . . into the kitchen and see if Aunt Laramie has any juice boxes in the fridge."

Since I often confused Dixie for a rat rather than a dog, I understood Daisy's need for reassurance on her species. I nodded at Owen to follow the boys. Aunt Laramie didn't have any juice boxes in her refrigerator, but Owen would find them something among the goodies in the saloon.

Owen sighed again, loudly, before leading the boys through the door to the kitchen. He is the nosiest person imaginable, not to mention the biggest gossip. He wanted to be in the know, not shuffled off to ride herd on two small boys and the rambunctious dogs. I watched him go, realizing that I already owed him big-time for the last two weeks. I would have to find some way to show him how important he was to me.

Then I turned to Daisy. "Okay, what's going on?"

3

OH, WHAT A TANGLED WEB WE WEAVE

I considered offering Daisy a chair—she looked like she was ready to drop (or to pop). But I needed answers, and maybe the quickest way to get them was to withhold some creature comforts.

"Laramie." Daisy's eyes welled with tears. "The boys and I need to stay here tonight. I was going to drive back to Montana this evening, but I just can't make it."

"Well, sure. You are family," I responded. "But why didn't you stay in Faith? Did you and Monty have a fight?" I hadn't even known she was in town. I wasn't that close to my family on the best of days, and being a newbie vampire had been just another reason to keep my distance over the last two weeks.

"Monty doesn't know I'm here. At The Madam, or even in Texas," she added, "and you can't tell him. My safety depends on it. Please let us stay tonight. I promise we'll be out of your hair first thing tomorrow morning." The tears she'd been holding back ran down her cheeks.

I have no defense against waterworks. Against my better judgment, I gave in. "Daisy, you and the boys are welcome to stay here tonight, but I don't feel right about Monty not knowing. Do you promise to tell him soon?"

She nodded. I didn't think there was a scrap of truth behind that head bob, but it was enough for me to hang my hat on if circumstances forced me to tell Monty myself. And tell him I would, if Daisy didn't. But not tonight.

Then I remembered. "Uh, Daisy, one thing. I'm having a Halloween party. Friends and people from the neighborhood—"

"Will your family be here?" Daisy interrupted. She clutched her bag in front of her as if to ward off an attack. Terror filled her eyes, and she looked like a deer about to bolt.

"No, no," I soothed. "At least, I don't think so. I invited them, but Monty wouldn't come and you know Mama and Cheyenne's stance on The Madam."

Daisy nodded. It was no secret that Mama and my sister Cheyenne thought I was crazy to take on The Madam and try to turn it into a business. When I inherited the house, Mama told me in no uncertain terms that I should sell it and stay in my hometown of Faith. She claimed there was no point in bankrupting myself trying to start a business when I had a secure job working at the wine bar on the town square. Cheyenne agreed, and repeated their opinion to anyone who would listen. They had never even been to The Madam. They said they didn't want to encourage me. And wasn't that a crazy idea? Family members encouraging each other.

Daisy had lost the startled deer look, but still clutched her bag. Was she scared of Monty? Blindsided by her departure with the twins, Monty had torn up to Montana after her, but he wasn't a violent person. My brother had returned from that trip alone, a broken and defeated man. Had something happened that I wasn't aware of?

Before I could ask any more questions, Owen popped in and said, "I've got the boys and the dogs settled in the saloon. The trick-or-treaters and the guests should start arriving soon. Anything else you need me to do?"

Right on cue, The Madam's doorbell drowned out the end of his sentence.

"I have to hide the boys!" Daisy cried.

I caught her arm. "I'll get the boys. Go up these stairs." I pointed at what had originally been the servants' staircase. "It will take you to my apartment on the third floor. You and the boys make yourselves comfortable there—it's more spacious than the second-floor bedrooms and it's off limits to guests tonight."

"I need to hide my car," she protested. "Can I park it in the shed out back?"

I hesitated. This was more serious than I'd realized.

"Give me the keys, and I'll put it the shed," Owen told Daisy. "Then I'll be up to get you and the boys settled."

Daisy sagged against the back door while she rummaged in her bag for the car keys. The doorbell tolled again, so I turned and made my way through the kitchen. Daisy and I were going to have a long talk tonight after my guests left, whether she wanted to or not.

4

IT'S PARTY TIME

My hope that the offer of free wine would help people overlook the recent murder had been right. I think the entire neighborhood was inside The Madam. The party was barely underway, and I'd already had to make a trip to the storeroom for more wine.

If I were still human, I'd have needed to wipe the sweat off my forehead when I set the wooden case filled with bottles of Texas reds on the bar. But with my new superhuman strength, the case of wine was as light as a feather. I'd just pretended it was heavy. I'd also tried to look like I was rushing, when in fact I'd slowed down to appear human. More importantly, I'd had to avoid brushing against anyone as I wove in and out of the crowded room. If I accidentally bumped into someone, at best they would notice I felt hard and cold, and at worst it could knock them to the ground. Battering my visitors wouldn't be the most auspicious start to my new business, and it definitely wouldn't help the insurance premiums that were already through the roof.

I was distracted from my vampire struggles by two small ghosts chasing a pint-sized stormtrooper and an equally diminutive Yoda across the bar area. The two spirits suspiciously matched the size of my twin nephews. I opened a variety of bottles of red wine and left them under the counter to breathe, then restocked the whites in the large ice buckets placed strategically along the bar.

The Whine Barrel wasn't officially open—two more days, I thought, knocking superstitiously on the wooden bar—so this was a private party. Bernie Wallach, the community activist who'd been murdered in my house a few weeks ago, had held up my final city code inspection just days before his death. But after the Cabernet Cavalry linked fellow vampire and Council Member Austin Crockett to Bernie's murder, my final paperwork sailed through the approval process. Crockett was in the wind, now, and good riddance to him.

Anyway, since it was a private party I could just leave the open bottles out on the bar and let everyone help themselves. I hoped the free-flowing wine would create a friendly atmosphere that would encourage the attendees to come back when I was charging for drinks. And, just as importantly, for them to pass the word about my new business along to their friends. I trusted most of the people in attendance tonight to monitor themselves, but I would keep an eye out for any over-imbibers, just in case.

Wine sorted, I started around the end of the bar to slow down the small visitors before they dashed into a table or knocked someone over. Before I could reach them, Owen stepped in front of the stormtrooper and corralled the four of them. Bo and Dixie, hot on their trail, joined the group. Bo grinned, and her big pittie tongue lolled out of one side of her mouth. Dixie grabbed the hem of the sheet covering one ghost and tugged on it for all she was worth. Casper gripped the sheet in one hand to keep it from being pulled off him, while his other kept a death grip on his candy. I hoped those ghosts weren't my nephews. It would be a long night for Daisy and me if they ingested that much sugar.

I reached them just as Owen patted Yoda on his green,

wrinkled head and pointed the group to the heavily laden food table we had set up along one wall of the saloon. I didn't know if the cakes and cookies were a better option than the candy, but at least it kept them from running through the crowd of people holding wine glasses.

"By any chance are those two ghosts related to me?" I asked Owen.

"And wouldn't you be having the right of it!" he responded in an accent that called to mind the Lucky Charms leprechaun.

I laughed despite myself. "Don't let Grace hear you talking like that!" Grace's lovely Irish accent made even the most common statement sound like poetry.

"True," he said in his normal voice. "As for the boys, they were excited about the party and I didn't think Daisy would get a bit of rest locked up with the two of them. After I rustled up some old sheets and cut holes for eyes, she agreed to let them come down for a while."

"Good thinking." Owen never ceased to amaze me.

The doorbell rang. "Rock, paper, scissors?" I asked, ready to battle it out. As owner of The Madam it was my duty to answer the door, but I was feeling nervous. What if it was Van? What if it wasn't? What if he didn't show up?

A tall figure in a floor length cape of midnight-black velvet stepped inside without waiting for anyone to open the door.

"Oh, my. Oh, my, my, my," Owen said in a deep voice. He set off through the packed saloon to the front door.

My, my, my was right. The cloak's hood concealed the new arrival's face, but the body the sumptuous fabric draped over, catching in all the right places, was utterly female.

The alluring guest pushed the hood back and Owen stopped in his tracks, his mouth open. It takes a lot to steal Owen's speech from him. I recognized the guest and moved closer. This was going to get better. The newcomer's hair glowed honey blond under The Madam's lighting and her blue eyes glittered from between impossibly long lashes. Based on her sun-kissed cheeks, the stunning socialite had recently returned from somewhere tropical.

"Laramie!" Bunny exclaimed as I arrived at the door, propelling a spellbound Owen the last few feet. "I love it. All of it!" She swept one arm around to indicate The Madam and unfastened the clasp of the cape, letting the garment slip from her shoulders like a drape being released to unveil an exquisite piece of art.

"Gralgle . . ." was all that Owen could manage at the sight of Bunny's statuesque body, scantily covered by a pink sateen Playboy Bunny costume. She had eschewed the bunny ears in favor of a black velvet headband.

"Why, Bunny Anderson, as I live and breathe," I said in my best Southern belle drawl. In the same way that Van's sister struck men speechless, she brought out the silly side I rarely trotted out. You would think I should hate such a fascinating woman, but truthfully, up until I realized that her brother, Van, was my one true love, she'd always been my favorite Anderson. "Owen, meet Abigail Anderson, better known to friends and family as Bunny. She's Van's sister."

"Hi, Bunny! And I thought Laramie's costume was on the nose." Then he gaped at me, horrified at his slip.

"Oh, not to worry, I know all about Laramie's little, ah, situation," Bunny said with a wink. She turned to me, lowered her voice and added, "and darling, I must say, you look marvelous."

I laughed. Bunny always knew just what to say and how to say it.

"Thanks. Is, uh, did anyone, well, did you bring a date?" I asked lamely. Unlike Bunny, I never knew how to say what I wanted.

"No, I came by myself." She took a moment to brush off the velvet cape that Owen had rescued from the floor. After what seemed an eternity, she looked up at me and the twinkle in her eyes gave her away. "But Van is coming. He's picking up LaRue on his way. Just wait until you see his costume."

I pressed, but she refused to say more about Van or his costume. "Just wait for it." Then she took Owen's arm and asked him to show her The Madam.

I tried not to do a happy dance right there beside the door. Van was coming! There was that tingle again, and I shivered in anticipation. But the fact that LaRue Landry would be with him doused my giddiness. LaRue is the self-proclaimed Voodoo Princess member of the Cabernet Cavalry. She owns a shop in Deep Ellum that carries the same name. LaRue and her voodoo ancestors have helped The Organization (that's what the Andersons / Van Helsings call their family business) fight bumpies for several generations. By the way, bumpies is how I refer to monsters. You know, things that go bump in the night?

LaRue doesn't like or trust vampires, but we'd established an uneasy truce, mostly for Van's sake, while we tried to stop me from turning into one. Our truce evaporated when I found out she had been my husband's mistress. My accidentally killing Van right after I changed sealed the deal. We were frenemies at best, sworn enemies at worst.

I pushed LaRue from my thoughts and imagined Van's handsome face lighting up at the sight of me. His blond hair would glow in The Madam's soft lighting, his Wedgwood blue eyes would glitter with excitement, and the small wrinkles around them would crease from the force of his smile. I fluffed my hair and wondered if I had time for a quick trip to the bathroom to check that my fake blood hadn't smeared. I hadn't been sure he would show tonight. Van loved me, I knew that, but he was having a hard time accepting my change into a vampire. His prejudice against supernatural beings was understandable—after all, his family had hunted them for centuries, and they had raised him to carry that pitchfork. But the biggest hurdle was that when he looked at me, he saw his own failure staring back. He felt guilty about what had happened to me. He and Jad had been friends since college. They'd joined the Dallas Police Department together and fought both bumpies and bad-guy humans alike. Van had promised Jad that he would always look after me if something happened to Jad, and he took that promise seriously. He believed he'd first failed to protect me from the supernaturals and then failed to save me from The Change. It didn't help that Van Helsing Anderson had failed at very few things in his life. He had no idea how to deal with it.

I watched Bunny and Owen cross the saloon, shaking my head at the Playboy Bunny and garish leprechaun. I placed my hand over my heart, moved by how wonderful my life had become in the last few weeks. Before I could get too sentimental, someone rapped on the door. Anticipation trilled through me. I turned to it with a broad smile and swung it open.

"Hey Bill," I said, trying valiantly to keep the smile plastered on my face. "Please, come on in." He waved a stunning woman into the house ahead of him.

"Laramie, this is my wife, Gabrella." Bill was the contractor who'd renovated The Madam. During my investigation into Bernie Wallach's murder, I'd discovered that Bill was having an affair with a much younger woman named Tiffany. He'd sworn to me he loved Gabrella and was going to end it with the young chickie before his wife found out, but I didn't know if he had.

"Hello, Gabrella," I said politely, but my thoughts were reeling. From past conversations with Bill, I knew that he and Gabrella were in their mid-forties. But she looked at least ten years younger and was gorgeous in a sexy, sultry kind of way. If someone would cheat on her, what hope was there for the rest of us? "It's so nice to finally meet you. We've spoken so many times on the phone, it's hard to believe that we've never met."

"Uh, huh." Gabrella looked me up and down with a hard stare.

Confused by her coldness, I kept gushing. "I'm so happy with the work that Martinez Construction has done at The Madam. Bill, please be sure to show Gabrella around. She'll be proud of all you've accomplished here."

"It's nice to know that Bill has the run of the place," she responded with a raised eyebrow.

Oh, crap! Gabrella must have figured out that Bill was involved in some hanky-panky, and pinned the bimbo tag on me. How the heck could I fix this?

"Hi, y'all!" A voice called out from the porch.

Oh, crap! Crap, crap, crap!

"What are you doing here?" Bill and I asked Tiffany at the same time.

5

A SERPENT IN THE GARDEN

"Well, hey Bill! Imagine my surprise when Mateo told me who he worked for on our way here. How's the running going?"

Tiffany, Bill's young chickie, stood on my threshold with Bill's foreman Mateo. Bill and Tiffany had met when she joined his running club. Despite her innocent expression, the odds of this being an accident were about equal to those of pigs flying.

Gabrella watched Tiffany and Mateo intently, her beautiful face as hard as granite, her lips pressed together so tightly that they turned white under their coat of crimson lipstick. I took an involuntary step back, removing myself from the crossfire between the two couples.

"The running is going well," Bill answered faintly.

"*Jefe.*" Mateo addressed Bill in Spanish. "Laramie, thank you for inviting us."

"Come in, come in. Mateo, I am so glad you could make it tonight," I said with a polite smile. As much as I didn't want Tiffany in my house, it would be awkward to make them stand outside. The gleeful grin Tiffany shot my way as she stepped across my threshold irked me. She was counting on me not making a scene.

Rather than let Tiffany piss me off, I focused on Mateo Montoya. He was young for a foreman, probably in his late twenties, but a hard worker. Word among The Madam's construction crew was that he played as hard as he worked. With his tall body, lean and well-muscled from years in construction, and his dark good looks, I believed the rumors.

As Mateo stepped through the threshold and moved past Gabrella, he whispered, "Hello, *Jefa*." She pretended not to hear, but glared at his back as he moved toward me. I was the only one who witnessed the exchange. Bill was busy staring at Tiffany, who was gazing around the saloon and pretending to ignore him.

Jefe and *Jefa* are Spanish for the masculine, and feminine of boss. Bill might be the brawn of Martinez Construction, but Gabrella was the brains. She ran the office and managed the paperwork. During The Madam's renovation, Bill's crew joked that he had to ask Gabrella's permission to buy so much as a new light bulb for a project. Bill took the ribbing good-naturedly and attributed the company's financial success to Gabrella's head for business.

Mateo introduced Tiffany to Gabrella and me, and Tiffany pretended it was the first time that we'd met. I went along with the pretense. Gabrella gave Tiffany the once-over with the same hard, suspicious demeanor she'd shown me. My heart ached for her. I knew firsthand how difficult it was to suspect that your husband is having an affair, but not knowing who with.

Tiffany laid her hand on Mateo's arm, batting her eyelashes at Bill. "I'm sure Laramie has hostessing duties to attend to, so why don't you two men show us around this big old house?" I glanced at the men to see how they reacted to her flirting and was surprised by the resemblance between the two. They both wore the typical Texas male party wear of starched blue jeans, pressed long-sleeved white shirts, and cowboy boots. But it went beyond the clothes. Mateo looked like a younger version of Bill.

They all seemed less than thrilled at Tiffany's request but turned and headed toward the kitchen as a group. Tiffany looked back, swinging her long, high-set ponytail over her shoulder, and the bitch smirked at me. She was up to something. I needed to figure out a way to get her out of The Madam before she set off World War III. For the sake of my future business, this party had to go off without a hitch.

I scanned the saloon for Owen, thinking I'd put him in charge of Tiffany damage control, but he was nowhere to be seen. He would have been easy to spot. His ridiculous leprechaun hat towered at least six inches over the heads of the other guests. Also not visible in the crowd were the Playboy Bunny, the small twin ghosts, and the dogs. No doubt Owen was giving Bunny the grand tour, with the boys and dogs tagging along. I hoped he had at least made the boys leave the candy behind.

Tiffany and company had stopped at the bar to fortify themselves with drinks before the tour. She was talking animatedly to Mateo while Bill poured them each a glass of wine. God, she was bad enough sober; it was not a good idea to give her alcohol. If only I could kill her and stuff her in the dumbwaiter until after the party. But no, that wouldn't do. I would just have to keep an eye on her. In the meantime, the cheese trays were getting dangerously low. I strode toward the kitchen, reminding myself to keep to a human pace.

I was almost to the swinging door when I heard the front doorbell chime again. Hoping it was Van, I spun and sped back to the door.

6

THE BUCKSTER

It wasn't Van. "Don! Come in, and this must be Buck." Once again, I held my welcome smile firmly in place, hiding my disappointment.

Don Williams was the City of Dallas code inspector who had been with me when we found Bernie's body. After I was cleared of Bernie's murder, Don came back and The Madam passed the code inspection with flying colors. It's amazing how not having a dead body in your house speeds up the process.

"This is the Buckster himself," Don replied as he stepped through the door, grinning his wide smile at me and holding out a small white poodle for my inspection.

"Don't call him that," someone said laughingly, "and you should introduce your wife before the dog."

A tall, elegant woman stepped into The Madam on Don's heels. Her shoulder-length salt-and-pepper dreadlocks were pulled into a low ponytail, and her bright smile, a perfect match for Don's, let me know that she was unconcerned about who got introduced first.

"Laramie, meet my better half and the woman who has been keeping me in line for over thirty years, my lovely wife Cheryl." Don's line sounded well-used, but the fond light in his eyes when he gazed at his wife proved that he meant every word.

"I've heard so much about you," I said to Cheryl. I couldn't resist adding, "and Buck."

"That's okay, I know who gets first billing." Cheryl laughed and put her arm through Don's affectionately.

Unbidden, a wave of envy moved through me. Here was a couple who had been together for years and still loved and admired each other. It was what I wanted, and I wanted it with Van. I tousled Buck's curls and he licked my hand in thanks.

"I hear your gift shop has the most darling dog sweaters. Buck gets so cold in the winter."

"Cheryl, Laramie isn't even open for business," Don said, shaking his head. "My wife can turn any situation into a shopping event."

"I'm so sorry," I said, mentally kicking myself. "I'm not set up for sales tonight."

"Perfect," Cheryl replied with a broad smile. "That means we'll have to return sooner rather than later. Is it okay if we look around?"

"Sure, what's your poison? I'll get you some wine and catch up with you. Also, Bo is around here somewhere. Give Buck free rein to find her, if you're comfortable with that."

"Surprise us," Don responded as he set Buck on the floor.

While I poured Don and Cheryl glasses of an earthy red tempranillo that I hoped would become a favorite with my future customers, I scanned the saloon. Bill and Tiffany's foursome were gone, probably touring the house. Although, with the room comfortably full of party goers, about half of them in costume, I might simply have lost them in the crowd. I loved that my friends and neighbors had gotten into the spirit of things.

I made a mental note to do a quick sweep to check on Tiffany after I dropped off the wine to Don and Cheryl. I couldn't put my finger on what was off about her, aside from her floozy ways, but something was. I didn't trust her.

Glasses in hand, I spotted Don and Cheryl stepping into one of the two small sunrooms that opened off the far wall and headed in their direction. Originally, The Madam's porch had wrapped around the front and both sides of the house, then had been closed off into separate sunrooms accessible by French doors from the sitting room and dining room. During renovations, I'd formed the saloon by combining The Madam's large front foyer, her formal dining room, and the sitting room into one large open area. So now the sunrooms opened directly into the saloon, and were the perfect size for an intimate dinner or small group gathering.

The front door opened again as I hurried toward Don and Cheryl, prepared to shove the wine at them and make quick excuses so I could greet Van. But the sight of the new arrivals had me diving into the sunroom with them for cover.

Mama, Daddy, and my sister, Cheyenne, had just walked into my home.

PARTY CRASHERS

"Laramie?" Cheryl asked tentatively, her forehead puckered in concern.

Lord, she must have thought I'd lost my mind. I stepped away from the wall I had flattened myself against and held out the wine, still sloshing precariously in the glasses. At least I hadn't spilled any.

"Sorry, my family just arrived. I didn't expect them to show up," I blurted out, then bit my lip. Someone as friendly and as open as Cheryl couldn't possibly understand my family dynamic.

But she nodded sympathetically and murmured, "Nobody can hurt you like family." Her eyes swept the room. "Don," she said firmly, "stand in the doorway, so Laramie has someone to hide behind." As Don placed himself like a linebacker in the opening, she took both glasses from my trembling hands, passed one to him, and took a sip of wine. "Oh, what is this? It's lovely. We're going to want a few bottles of it when you open," she said, as if I hadn't just acted like a crazy woman. I liked this lady.

While Cheryl and Don discussed the wine's notes and

scents, I peeked around Don's enormous frame to check my family's location.

Mama, Daddy, Cheyenne, and my two nieces were standing in a tight group in the middle of the saloon, shifting uncomfortably. Of all the nights for my family to support me! I needed to get out there and keep them from wandering through the house. I couldn't let them find Daisy. I had put up ropes across the stairs to the third floor earlier to politely dissuade guests from going into my personal area. Unfortunately, Mama and Cheyenne have never been ones to let a little thing like politeness keep them from doing anything they wanted to. Now that they had deigned to enter The Madam, they would want to go through every inch of her.

An even worse thought struck me: Monty's boys were running around the house. My family might not recognize the twins in their ghost costumes, but there was no way the twins wouldn't recognize them.

I was turning back to Don and Cheryl to excuse myself when I saw the front door swing open. The latest arrival was in full costume, and my lips curled into a smile. Although a chain mail hood concealed his head and face, it had to be Van. The newcomer was Van's height and build and the Knights Templar costume—a white tunic with a square red cross on its chest—was a nod to his tendency to be my knight in shining armor. Owen had even joked that the only thing Van lacked was a white horse. Now I knew why Bunny was so taken with his costume. It was perfect.

Van hurried across the saloon and into the kitchen before I could intercept him. Surprisingly, he passed my family without stopping to talk. He'd been close to them since Jad died, especially my brother Monty. Or since we'd all *thought* Jad died. That was probably it. He didn't want to talk to them in case he gave away the fact that Jad was alive, or sort of alive. I'd stayed away from them myself for the last two weeks—although that was nothing new for me.

The front door opened again. Who'd have thought this many people would show up to support me? My cold, motionless heart warmed with pleasure for the second time that night.

A beautiful woman I didn't recognize stepped inside and looked around. She wore a red cloak similar to Bunny's black one, but its material rested behind her shoulders, superhero style, revealing a crimson dress so skimpy it was barely this side of scandalous. My warm feeling fled. If the costume was her take on Little Red Riding Hood, she was missing a basket and a lot of clothing. I've never liked how some women use Halloween as a chance to dress slutty. Or perhaps I'm jealous of their abandon. Before coming downstairs tonight, I had safety-pinned the plunging neckline of my dress into a much more modest V-neckline.

After surveying the saloon, she started up the grand staircase. Something about her struck me as strange, besides the fact that she hadn't made a beeline to the free booze. I had made it clear to guests they were welcome to wander the first two floors to see the renovations, but normally people would get a drink and some food first. I mean, who passes up free hooch? And how did she know it was okay to visit the other floors? She was acting pretty bold, if you asked me.

I needed to search for the boys. If I could slip across the saloon and up the stairs unnoticed by my family, I could keep an eye out for the twins and monitor my mystery guest at the same time. I moved to follow her, then remembered Don and Cheryl. How rude must they think me?

"I'm sorry." I turned back to them, smiling. "I need to check on the food and wine, but please make yourselves at home. Thank you so much for coming tonight, and I hope to see you back here real soon."

Cheryl smiled. "Laramie, we wouldn't have missed it. I've been wanting to see inside this old house ever since Don told me about it." After a pointed look at Don, she added, "And I will reach out to you this week to talk about having Don's retirement party here."

"Retirement!" I burst out. Don groaned.

"Don hasn't made this widely known yet, but he submitted his retirement paperwork to the city this week. He won't be a code inspector much longer."

"Don! Congratulations!" I said. "Unfortunately, the city is losing a good one with you. I'd be honored to hold your party here. In fact, I'll open a bottle of sparkling wine and we'll toast your plans."

"I appreciate the offer, but I'm trying to keep it low key," Don said, looking at the floor. "I just couldn't keep working there after my supervisors allowed the code department to be used as a political pawn in your inspection."

"I understand," I said, and I did. Council member Austin Crockett had used his position to manipulate my code inspection timing, so that Don would find the murdered activist Bernie Wallach's body in my dumbwaiter. Crockett had disappeared since then, and a new person was temporarily filling his seat. But when you worked in city government, especially Dallas, there were constant shenanigans. I didn't blame Don for wanting to be out of it, but I hated that he was so disillusioned he didn't want to celebrate his retirement.

"Well, I for one won't turn down a glass of sparkling wine." Cheryl turned to Don. "And you had an amazing career. We deserve to celebrate its highlights and toast your retirement."

With a wife like Cheryl, Don wouldn't look back on his career with regret for very long. She wouldn't let him.

"Okay, I need to do a sweep through the house. I'll snag a bottle from the wine chiller in the stockroom and rejoin the party. Give me about fifteen minutes and then meet me by the bar." I needed to check the saloon and the rest of the house for my nephews and herd them up to Daisy before they ran into their grandparents or cousins. I also needed to find Van, and make sure the slutty Little Red Riding Hood didn't get up to mischief in my home.

There were only two routes around my family: I could slip into the kitchen and then head up the back stairs or slink across the saloon and up the grand staircase. I decided on the second option, mainly because my family was congregated in front of the kitchen door. The main stairs would put me on display to everyone in the saloon, but once I started up them it would be hard for my family to catch up with me.

8

ONE BIG HAPPY FAMILY

I was only a few feet from the bottom of the grand staircase. If I could reach it without my family noticing me, I would be home free, at least for a while. I should have known it was too good to be true. Just as I passed the front door, another guest entered The Madam.

I couldn't exactly ignore her. "Hello, welcome to The Whine Barrel," I said, fighting my urge to sweep past her and run up the stairs.

She turned large, copper-colored eyes to me, and I felt a jolt of recognition, along with something else. Try as I might, I couldn't place her or the odd sensation. Was she a neighbor? Her long, forest-green cloak covered her body and its hood concealed her hair. What was it with cloaks tonight?

"Thank you. Your home is beautiful," she said. "I've wanted to see the inside for a long time."

Dang! Even her voice sounded familiar. Who was she? Now I didn't feel right asking her name. Maybe she thought I knew her. "Well, I am glad you stopped by," I said. "The first and second floors are open to visitors. Please feel free to wander."

"Thank you." She looked around her and then, like the

previous guest, moved up the grand staircase without first getting a drink from the bar. Weirder and weirder. Were the cloaked ladies having a convention up there?

"Laramie!"

I'd know my mama's voice anywhere. I wanted to pretend I hadn't heard her, but I'd been caught and would have to pay the price. I turned slowly, taking a couple of seconds to gather my wits. There was no way I could get out of greeting my family now. I trudged back across the saloon toward the three adults and two small princesses who waited for me by the kitchen door.

Daddy's face lit up when his gaze landed on me, while Mama and Cheyenne looked at me bug-eyed. Becoming a vampire had subtly changed my looks for the better. My stick-straight brown hair had gained thickness and body. My skin was smooth and unblemished. But more than the cosmetic changes, I now had a spark that seemed to draw people's eyes to me, although that might have been from the confidence I'd gained during the days before The Change. Whatever the cause, the reflection that stared out at me from the mirror was better than before I'd become a bumpy. (By the way, I use that term a lot. It sounds less formal than "supernatural" and more appealing than "undead." Oh, and yes, my reflection appears in mirrors. I have no clue where that myth got started.)

Despite the changes, most people didn't notice the difference. The bottom line is—and this is a sad reflection on us as human beings—we don't really see others. We carry around a picture of them in our heads, and unless there is a drastic change, we view only the picture, not the reality.

But Mama and Cheyenne aren't most people, at least not where I'm concerned. Oh, don't think I'm giving them credit for looking beyond what normal people see. It's simply that they are super-critical of me. They both spend a small fortune on hairstyles, color, highlighting, facials, mani-pedis, and makeup. Basically, the works. With their perfectly dyed and highlighted blond locks and matching facial expressions, they looked more like twins than mother and daughter. By contrast, I don't spend much on my appearance and I never have. I'm not against it, I just don't have the time or money to fool with anything beyond a basic haircut and a few swipes of drugstore makeup. But to hear either of them tell it, I don't have the sense to dress myself before going out in public. So whenever they see me they are like heat-seeking missiles, targeting my shortcomings.

For once, I savored their disgruntled looks. Their mouths puckered as if they were sucking on lemons.

"Hey y'all," I said to the group, unable to restrain the wide smile stretching across my face. "And what kingdoms do you two reign over?" I asked, dropping to one knee to address Cheyenne's daughters, Amber and Avery. They wore the requisite princess dresses that covered almost every little girl their ages on Halloween—and many other nights of the year too, if Cheyenne's Instagram account was anything to go by.

"Ice!" Avery, the youngest of the two, squealed.

"Texas," Amber replied regally. She, like her mother, dreamed big.

"Well, I'm sure it thrills your subjects to have such beautiful monarchs." At their puzzled looks I added, "princesses." They giggled in unison.

"Laramie, Monty has told us this place was amazing," Daddy said, "but I still wasn't expecting it to be this nice. And so full of your friends!" When I stood, I saw that he was a little misty-eyed. The pride on his face put a lump in my throat. He kissed my cheek and then, overcome, wrapped me in an embrace. "Brrr!" He drew back immediately and took off his jacket, draping it over my shoulders. "Have you been outside? You're as cold as death."

"Well, if the girl would wear some clothes . . ." Mama said, eyeing the shallow V-neck of my long-sleeved, floor length dress, which exposed only slightly more skin than a nun's habit. "And of course people are going to overrun the place when she's giving alcohol away for free. I swear, Laramie, you're going to bankrupt yourself before you ever serve your first paying customer."

"Now, Josie, it's a party," Daddy admonished her.

Time to change the subject. "Where are Monty and Bradley?" I handed Daddy his jacket back with a small smile. I wasn't really expecting either of the men to come tonight. Monty hadn't been out much since Daisy left him. Bradley, Cheyenne's long-suffering husband—the way I imagined him, at least—hadn't been at a family function in . . . Well, I couldn't actually remember the last one he'd been at.

"There they are!" Cheyenne pointed toward the kitchen.

Dread filled me when my gaze landed on Monty and Bradley weaving toward us through the crowded saloon. I tried to keep my eyes focused on them rather than looking for the twins, but it was hard to maintain my self-control.

"Hey! I'm so glad y'all could come!" I exclaimed, giving first Monty and then Bradley hard hugs, while looking frantically over their shoulders for the ghosts. "Did you come in the back?"

I caught a whiff of an odd, faint odor that I couldn't place.

"Yes," Monty said. "I had to park several blocks away. I was lucky enough to find a spot right by Bradley's truck and then caught up with him in the backyard."

"Yeah, apparently people come from all over Dallas to trick-or-treat in this neighborhood." I couldn't quell my pride in The Madam and her surroundings. "It has a reputation for being very safe."

"I don't know about that," Monty responded with a frown. "When I was walking up, I heard firecrackers close by. That's not a good idea with all the kids running around."

"Really?" Fireworks at Halloween in this kid-conscious neighborhood surprised me. There had been some bangs and whistles the night of the Fourth of July, but that was to be expected. Then I noticed that acrid scent in the air, again. "Now that you mention it, I do smell something like . . . gunpowder?"

"Oh, that would be me, not the firecrackers," Monty said sheepishly. "I spent the afternoon out at the deer lease, shooting targets. I needed to get away and blow off some steam. I can't believe it stuck to me like that. I changed clothes and washed my hands, I swear."

"Well, no . . ." I trailed off, unable to explain that I'd only detected it because of my improved vamp senses. Better not open that can of worms. "Bradley, why didn't you ride with Cheyenne?"

"I had to stop by Anna's after I left the dealership. She needed some things done around the house. It's hard for her to do much in her condition."

Over Bradley's shoulder I saw Cheyenne roll her eyes at Mama. No surprise, Mama returned it.

"Oh, poor thing. She's lucky to have such a considerate brother. How is her pregnancy going?" I asked Bradley innocently, unable to resist an opportunity to aggravate Mama and Cheyenne at the same time.

Anna is Cheyenne's sister-in-law. Probably because Anna and Bradley were just teenagers when their parents died, they are exceptionally close. They also comanage the Ford dealership in Faith that they inherited—or they had, until Anna became pregnant. She'd experienced complications, and the doctor put her on bed rest several months back. Since then, running the business and taking care of Anna had fallen solely on Bradley. Anna and Cheyenne viewed each other as contenders for Bradley's attention, so there was no love lost between them. That they were cut from the same cloth didn't help matters. I felt bad for Bradley being caught between those two needy, demanding, slightly psychotic . . . but I digress.

"She's managing okay," Bradley replied, but the deepening of the worried crease between his eyebrows made me wonder. "I'm taking her to Arkansas to see our grandmother tomorrow."

"Should she be traveling in her state?" Mama's disapproving tone had more to do with Anna being single and having refused to name the father than any genuine concern for her wellbeing.

Cheyenne clapped her hands. "Now that we are all together, I have a little announcement to make that I think will liven this party right up." She couldn't stand not being the center of attention.

I gritted my teeth and was on the verge of pointing out that the party was full of people having a wonderful time, when I noticed Cheyenne clutch Bradley's hand in hers. She was smiling, but she bit her bottom lip anxiously, looking nervous and a little afraid. I'd only ever seen Cheyenne look this way when she and Bradley had—

OH, BABY! PART 2

"I'm pregnant!" Cheyenne exclaimed.

—told my parents the first time she was pregnant. She had been eighteen, and it was before they got married. Before they planned to get married, as far as I knew.

Shocked looks blanketed the surrounding faces. Even Mama, whom Cheyenne usually told everything, looked stunned. And something else—a little dubious? But do you know who looked the most surprised? Bradley, the father—or the alleged father—looked downright flabbergasted. I fought the urge to look down at Amber, Cheyenne's oldest daughter. I'm still not convinced she's his.

Then a pink mist crept over my vision. This was my party. My family had finally come to The Madam, yet Cheyenne couldn't let me have the spotlight for even two minutes.

One, two, three. I focused on counting. Grace had told me it would help when the rages threatened to overtake me. Heightened emotions, along with heightened senses, were a part of the vampire blessing—or curse, depending on how you looked at it.

Mama was the first to recover. With a low squeal, she

threw her arms around Cheyenne and pulled her into a tight hug. I couldn't remember the last time Mama had hugged me. Four, five, six.

Cheyenne's eyes met mine over Mama's shoulder, and I saw an emotion in them I rarely witnessed from my sister. She looked apologetic. But before I could process it, Mama turned from her to me. I thought in her excitement she was going to hug me and lifted my arms, preparing for the embrace.

"Laramie! Why are you just standing there? Surely you have some champagne somewhere in this place so we can toast your sister. This is supposed to be a wine bar, isn't it?"

The haze over my vision deepened from pink to light red. As much as I wanted to explain the difference between Champagne and Texas sparkling wine, I needed to get away from Mama more. I moved toward the kitchen without a word. Seven, eight, nine.

I stepped through the swinging door from the saloon into the kitchen, still struggling for control. The sight of Bill Martinez and Tiffany huddled in conversation with their wineglasses resting on the kitchen island did nothing to improve the thin grip I held on my temper. Ten, eleven, twelve.

I glared at Bill. I did not need another murder in The Madam, preferably ever, and if that wasn't attainable, definitely not so close on the heels of the last one. But, hand to God, if Gabrella didn't kill Bill, I might, if he didn't get the heck away from Tiffany. I would not allow these two yahoos to ruin my party. Thirteen, fourteen, fifteen.

As if reading my mind, Bill snatched up his wineglass and hurried through the kitchen's rear door into the small misshapen foyer I call the mudroom. He couldn't have chosen a better door. The Madam's back door, the rear staircase, a door to my office, and the door to the stockroom all opened into the area. Multiple escape routes were open to him.

The red haze receded a touch, at least until I took in Tiffany's petulant look, then it kicked right back up. What number had I been up to? *Oh, crap!* One, two, three.

I paused for a moment and shot Tiffany what I hoped was the evil eye, but she only sneered at me in return. Figuring her a lost cause, I decided to catch up to Bill and give him what for. But when I entered the mudroom he was nowhere to be seen. I nearly collided with the twins and the three dogs. Buck had found Bo and Dixie, and they were getting on like gangbusters. Relief washed over me. I wouldn't have to search the entire house for the boys! Thoughts of chastising the disappearing Bill flew right out of my head.

"Aunt Laramie—" started one of the boys. I wasn't sure if it was Hayden or Harley. I couldn't tell them apart on a good day, much less with sheets covering them.

"Hayden, Harley, y'all go up and stay with your mother," I said to the sweet boys.

Make that the not-so-sweet boys. Even with their faces covered, I could tell that their expressions were mutinous. But they must have seen that I was in no mood for any back talk and let me herd them to the rear stairs and send them on their way. They dragged their feet up each stair and then slowly disappeared around the first bend in the staircase. The dogs followed, looking back at me reproachfully. It wasn't until they disappeared from view that I realized Dixie hadn't snapped at my ankles, or even growled.

"Laramie?"

I spun around to find Bradley and Monty watching me. Had they seen the twins?

"Hey, what are y'all doing back here?" I asked with only the slightest tremor in my voice.

"Mama sent us back to help you. She said not to skimp, that we will need several bottles to do this right," Monty said with a grimace.

Bradley smiled at me weakly. It might be because he owned a car dealership that people often joked that he stayed in salesman mode. But I'd found him friendly and down-to-earth with me when Cheyenne and he were first married. It was only after he realized his attention caused Cheyenne to be harder on me that he became reserved. It was too bad he'd gotten saddled with my sister besides his own.

"How are you doing, Bradley?" I asked softly. Cheyenne dropping this news on him in front of the rest of us was callous, even for her.

"I'm . . . excited," he replied, trying to hold his weak smile in place.

I pulled my set of keys from the pocket of my dress as I turned to open the storeroom door.

"Hey, maybe it will be a boy this time. You've always wanted a boy . . ." When Monty's voice trailed off, I knew he was thinking of his sons.

I turned to see Bradley nodding at him, then catching himself. "I just hope it's healthy."

It was a nice effort, but the entire family knew Bradley wanted a boy more than he could breathe. When I looked at Monty, his face had collapsed in on itself. I felt horrible. He missed Daisy and the boys so much. Really, what would it hurt for me to tell him she was here? They needed to talk.

I vowed to tell him right after we toasted Cheyenne's baby, and then send him upstairs. I wouldn't let either of them leave until they talked things out.

Oh, how I wish I'd sent him upstairs right then and there.

Instead, I turned back to the storeroom door and grasped empty air where the padlock should have hung from its hasp. That wasn't good. After Bernie's murder, I discovered that my neighbor, Tom Harner, was using a secret tunnel to access The Madam. The dank passageway from the cellar of his house next door opened into a hidden room next to my cellar. I hadn't known about the hidden room—which I now affectionately call The Bat Cave—but both Van and Jad had. They'd used it as a headquarters and training room when they worked together fighting bumpies. The Organization's equipment and books still filled it. The Bat Cave opened into my cellar, whose steps led into the storeroom. I had taken to keeping the door padlocked.

But the lock was missing.

More than likely, Owen was in the storeroom getting wine for the party. He was the only other person with a key to the padlock. Owen had helped us cover up Tom's death in The Bat Cave. His lips were sealed regarding the secrets The Madam held under her skirts.

But what if it wasn't Owen in the cellar? Tom had been part of a larger plot that involved vampires, werewolves, and the search for the True Cross Owen had been nagging me about finding. I had no way of knowing who else Tom had told about The Bat Cave or the access route between our houses.

A child's high-pitched laughter drifted down the stairs, breaking into my reverie. I couldn't chance Bradley and Monty seeing whatever or whoever might be in the stockroom, and I surely couldn't risk the twins seeing them until I'd had a chance to tell Monty his ex-wife was here in the house. Which I couldn't do until I'd dealt with Cheyenne's baby celebration. This night was getting more and more complicated.

"Hey guys," I turned to address the men and found them looking up the back staircase. It hadn't just been my supernatural hearing; they had heard the laugher, too. "The lock is off the stockroom door, so Owen must be inside stocking up. Why don't you go back to the party? He can help me bring the wine out."

Monty and Bradley exchanged looks. It wouldn't be an easy sell. Mama had sent them to help, and she expected her orders followed. While they pondered what to do, I examined them both, surprised by how similar they looked. Like Bill and

Mateo, they and my daddy were in the Texas male party outfit. Their white starched shirts practically glowed in the dim light of the mudroom.

"Seriously guys, I've got this." Before they could answer I slipped into the storeroom and closed the door behind me.

STRANGERS IN THE NIGHT

The light was on in the storeroom. Other than the crates of wine and the large refrigerator in one corner, it was empty. When my gaze fell on the door that led into the cellar, my stomach dropped. The padlock I kept on that door was missing, too, and I possessed the only key.

I moved to the cellar door. Whoever was down there had closed it behind him. I stood, unmoving, and concentrated on my senses. A few indistinct noises reached me, but I couldn't tell where they came from. It could just be the scratching of the mice who lived in the walls, or it could be something more sinister. Next, I inhaled. The tangy odor of wine assailed me, but then I caught a trace of something else, a familiar scent that tickled some part of my brain. I should be able to place it, but like the woman in the cape, I couldn't quite put my finger on what it evoked.

The wooden steps that led from the cellar to the storeroom shifted and creaked. Without my supernatural hearing, I wouldn't have picked up the sounds. Someone, or something —a bumpy, perhaps!—was climbing the stairs. And he, she, or it was being stealthy.

Any second, the door was going to open and whatever had

been snooping around my cellar and I were going to have a throwdown. I considered my wine stock regretfully. Normally, I would rather have said throwdown anywhere except this room, but protecting my guests was my priority. I had to keep the intruder contained.

Grace and Marek had been promising me for the last two weeks that they would teach me how to be a vampire, including how to fight. I wished they had moved the lessons up.

The cellar door creaked open. I leaped backward a few feet to give us some fighting room and dropped into a crouch. When the Templar Knight emerged, I sagged with relief.

"Van!" I exclaimed and rushed toward him. I stopped short, leaving a few feet between us, and clasped my hands to keep from throwing my arms around him. A girl must maintain a scrap of dignity, right? "You scared me to death. I didn't know who was down there."

Being this close to Van changed my anxiety to longing. Longing for his hands to pull me against him. Longing for his mouth to close over mine. Longing . . . I have to tell you, all this longing was heating up parts of me that hadn't been warm in a long time—if you catch my drift.

As if Van read my mind, he closed the gap between us, stirring the air, and a whiff of the familiar smell tickled at my memories again. It called to mind hay and sunshine and horses—all things that were Van, but at the same time, not. Then, all thought of scents and memories went out of my head as he wrapped me in his arms and pulled me, hard, against his body. And y'all, his pull wasn't the only thing that was hard. Then all coherent thought left me when his mouth covered mine in a deep kiss that was . . . not Van.

We'd only kissed once, but I knew Van, and this wasn't him. Unfortunately, it took several seconds for my mind to override my senses.

"Jad!" I tried to exclaim, but he held me tighter and deepened the kiss. I struggled, but he'd trapped my arms. I contorted and twisted my body to create enough space between us to bring my hands up to his shoulders. Pausing, I gathered my strength to break the embrace.

"What the hell!" The harsh words came from the storeroom's door. Jad lifted his head, but didn't release me. I turned to the door, sending up a prayer to the romance gods that I hadn't correctly identified the outraged voice.

I had, and as if it wasn't bad enough that Van had caught me in a clinch with my vampire ex-husband, he wasn't alone.

Van stood blocking the doorway from the mudroom. Peering around him with horrified faces were Owen, Bunny, and LaRue.

"Van! This isn't what it looks like!" I exclaimed, then I wanted to slap myself for using the oldest 'caught cheating' line in the book.

I struggled to free myself from Jad and his arms dropped easily to his sides. He flashed his infuriating lopsided grin at me and casually leaned against a shelf loaded with bottles of wine. I knew that look. It was his 'let me see how you get out of this' expression.

I swear, at that moment, if I'd had a stake, I would have plunged it into his chest without a smidgeon of hesitation.

"Van—" I tried again, but was interrupted by a loud crash and screams from the saloon.

11

LET'S DANCE

Van and I locked eyes briefly, and then he spun toward the screaming. A long black cape billowed behind him as he sprinted from the stockroom doorway. Have I failed to mention that he was dressed as an old-fashioned vampire from the movies? I followed him, leaving Jad in the storeroom, flying past LaRue, Bunny, and Owen, and catching up in the kitchen. As we ran together to the saloon, I caught brief glimpses of the red satin lining of Van's cape as it swirled around him. I have to give credit to the Van Helsings: They do nothing half-assed. Bunny's high heels clattered behind me and, if I knew Owen, he would be on her tail, pun intended. I figured LaRue had stayed behind to stake Jad, or at least grill the hell out of him. I imagined how our little group would appear to a bystander—a Bela Lugosi vampire, a Mistress of the Night vampire, a Playboy Bunny and a leprechaun running through a house toward danger. We resembled the start of a dirty joke more than a rescue squad.

Van pushed through the swinging kitchen door and barreled into the saloon, only to slide to a screeching stop. I slammed into him. Bunny rammed into me and then Owen into her. Just call us the four stooges. Make that the five stooges, I thought, as another person rammed into the back of our group. So LaRue had stuck with us after all.

I peered around Van to see what had caused his reaction. The beautiful woman in the skimpy red dress who I'd dubbed Little Red Riding Hood, stood in the center of the room, plastic fangs on display. Her cloak was MIA. I'd been wrong; her costume for the night was slutty vampire. A low growl rumbled from her throat, followed by a hiss, and ice shot up my spine. Her fangs weren't from the dollar store. An honest-to-God vampire had crashed my party and was threatening my guests.

"Ora Lee," I heard Owen whisper. I gaped back at him, surprised that he knew her, but he wasn't looking at the slutty vampire in the middle of my wine-tasting room. He was looking at the vampire on my grand staircase.

What the hell? There were only supposed to be perhaps ten vampires in the entire world, me included, and I knew six of them. Again, me included. Had the rest of them decided to have a convention in my house? And how did Owen know one of them?

Then it clicked. The vampire on the stairs was the mysterious woman in the green cloak I hadn't been able to place earlier. Now she removed the cloak and tossed it over the staircase's banister, never taking her eyes off the slutty vampire. A black T-shirt, skinny jeans, and red canvas high tops encased her long, lithe body. Hair the same copper shade as Owen's swirled around her shoulders. Her eyes, the color of new pennies, were also an exact match of his.

Except for their genders and hairstyles, she and Owen were identical. But Owen's twin sister was dead, or supposed to be.

"I'll contain everyone," LaRue whispered, then slowly began weaving through the crowd.

Contain everyone? Shouldn't we be trying to get the humans out of the house? I scanned the faces of my guests.

Mama and Daddy were standing midway across the room, staring at my scantily clad party crasher. I moved to put myself between them and the vampire. While I had been pondering the mysteries of the vampire universe, my human guests had backed up against the walls of the saloon, leaving the slutty vampire alone in the middle of the room. But only one of them was brave enough, or stupid enough, to complain.

"Laramie, what the hell kind of party are you throwing?" Cheyenne asked disdainfully as she strode in from the kitchen. Where had she been?

The slutty vampire followed Cheyenne's gaze to me. Understanding flared in her hazel eyes, and as Cheyenne brushed past her, she grabbed my sister's throat. One-handed, she lifted Cheyenne, kicking and screaming, until her feet dangled several inches above the floor.

The vampire on the stairs yelled, "Star, let her go! She isn't part of this!"

Star?

"Where is he?" the slutty vampire, er, Star demanded of me. "You're hiding him somewhere in this house. Tell me or I'll kill her."

Who was she talking about? The only person I was hiding was Daisy, but she was a she, not a he.

"Time's up!" Star pulled back her free arm, ready to deck Cheyenne with a vampire punch that would permanently damage Cheyenne's perfect features. I flew into action. My sister was the bane of my existence, but if anyone got to kick her ass, it would be me.

I took two running steps and launched myself at Star. She barely shifted her stance and backhanded me in mid-air. I crashed into the wall that supported The Madam's grand staircase and shook my head to clear away the Tweety birds that circled above me.

Star still had a grip on Cheyenne's neck, and my sister's face had turned a livid red.

"Laramie, tell her what she wants to know!" Mama yelled at me. I looked over to where she and Daddy stood on the edge of the crowd. Daddy's fists were clenched, and I knew the only thing that had kept him out of the fight this long was that he didn't want to hit a woman.

"I don't know who she's talking about!" I yelled, as much at Star as Mama.

"Where is Jad?" Star demanded.

Finally, Van rushed forward, his cape flying behind him. Star threw Cheyenne into him and they fell in a tangled heap by the food table. I was pushing up onto my hands and knees when Star grasped my throat and slammed me back against the wall, pinning me there.

"Where is he?" she demanded again, her blood-red eyes boring into mine.

"Star!" Owen's vampire sister, Ora Lee, jumped from the staircase. She wound her hands in my attacker's hair and yanked her off of me. Like a snake twisting on its tail, Star turned on Ora Lee and shoved her several feet backwards. When she came to a stop, she held two handfuls of long black hair.

"You bitch!" Star frantically clutched her scalp, feeling for bald spots.

"Star! You need to leave!" Ora Lee yelled. "There is nothing for you here."

I pushed up, crossed the room in a single leap, and landed in a crouch between Star and my family. The simultaneous outraged gasps from Mama and Cheyenne proved what I already knew. I had moved faster than was humanly possible, and I had a maniac at my party. I would have a lot to answer for, later.

Make that two maniacs. The vampires circled each other in

the center of the saloon, hissing and growling. With their fangs extended and glowing red embers for eyes, they resembled rabid creatures straight out of nightmares. My guests pressed back against the walls. Or most of them did. Cheryl was clinging to Don's arm, trying to stop him from joining the fray. Don was huge, but he was no match for vampires. I looked around frantically, trying to figure out what to do. My gaze fell on the open front door and I got my first good look at LaRue, dressed as a voodoo priestess. She stood on The Madam's threshold, her tight black dress slit nearly to her waist. The dark circles she had painted around her eyes accentuated her amber irises and latte-toned skin. A small headdress—more a tiara, really, an artistic concoction of black feathers and small white bones—nestled in her ginger hair. Her normally perfect ringlets had been teased into a halo that made her look primitive and fierce. I would have to ask her to show me how she had done that. I mentally slapped myself. *Focus, Laramie!*

LaRue was murmuring and waving her hands. I knew from experience she was performing a ritual, but I didn't know what for.

Van positioned himself between the circling vampires and the guests who lined the bar.

"Stay away from us," Ora Lee hissed at Star.

"Make me," Star sneered.

"Ora Lee, stop!" Owen had pushed through the guests and reached out to her.

"Stay back!" Ora Lee rounded on Owen viciously.

Bunny, who must have been waiting for an opening, rushed at Ora Lee with a pointy wooden stake held high.

Where in that tiny Playboy Bunny outfit had she been hiding that? Her costume didn't look like it would conceal a tissue, much less a wooden stake. Nonetheless, Bunny had one, and she was hell bent on planting it in Ora Lee.

Van and Bunny move faster than normal humans because of genetic enhancement experiments Nazi scientists conducted on their grandfather in World War II. And with Ora Lee focused on Owen, Bunny was able to drive the stake down in a hard arc toward her chest.

It sunk into flesh. Human flesh. At the last possible moment, Owen had flung himself at his sister, using his body as a shield.

12

RESISTING TEMPTATION

"No!" Ora Lee screamed as Owen slid to the ground, the hilt of the stake protruding from his back.

Apparently, Star wanted no part of stake-wielding humans. She spun in a tight circle, looking for an escape route. Her only easy options were the front door, the door to the kitchen, or the grand stairs. I say easy because the other doors that led from the saloon—to the bathrooms, sunrooms, and gift shop—were either locked or dead ends. LaRue had blocked the front door, and guests crowded around the kitchen door, clutching each other in shock and fear.

Star gathered herself and leaped onto the grand staircase, landing just below the second floor. With a final hiss at us, she disappeared up the stairs.

A low moan drew my attention back to Owen. Ora Lee was on the floor and had pulled him into her lap. I dropped beside them. Oh God, oh God, oh God, it looked bad. I could hear his heart beating, but it was slowing down. A woozy feeling washed over me and his heart's throbbing reverberated in my head. I couldn't lose Owen. He was my best friend, the only person in the world I could truly count on. Oh, Jesus, my fangs were extending as his blood's earthy fragrance wafted around me. Coppery and spicy with just a hint of—

"Go after her!"

The order and the hard shove from Ora Lee brought me back to myself.

"Wha . . . ?" Well, maybe not completely back, but it broke the trance that Owen's blood and heartbeat had woven around me.

Ora Lee spoke quietly. "I can save him, but you have to stop her. Star is a killer. Don't let her escape." I believed her. On both counts.

I looked at the staircase. I didn't know how Star had made that leap, but I couldn't do it. I sped to the bottom stair, glancing at LaRue as I passed the front door. Her eyes were closed, her lips silently mouthing words. Using the ornately carved wooden ball that topped the sturdy newel post, I swung around the bottom of the stairs without losing momentum and launched myself toward the second floor.

When I reached the top step, I glanced back and saw Van following me in hot pursuit, his Dracula cape billowing behind him. A tingle ran through me. We were working together as a team. I glanced down at the saloon and was struck by the sense that I was floating above the scene. Bunny was huddled on the floor beside Ora Lee and Owen. My guests, their faces filled with horror, pressed around them. Most of the people who mattered to me were either in that room or somewhere in this house—one of them mortally injured—and I had a deranged vampire on the loose.

Meanwhile, Star had disappeared. The bedrooms on the second floor were unlocked for the guests to view. She could be in any room on that floor, or she might have gone up to the third floor, or she could have taken the rear staircase down to the back door.

I sniffed for her scent. The odor of Owen's blood permeated the air, overpowering any trace of Star. In fact, the fragrance was stronger up here, and somehow different. It had taken on a dark and slightly mysterious essence, like vanilla mixed with clove.

Was it even Owen's blood? Since The Change, I had only smelled Van's blood and some in a cup that Grace tried to get me to drink. Did each person's blood have a distinctive odor?

"Stop it! Leave her alone!" someone yelled from the rear of the house.

I ran along the second-floor corridor toward the sound, and y'all, the sight that greeted me stopped me in my tracks. Star knelt over a woman's body, her mouth attached to the prostrate victim's neck. Tiffany was pressed against the wall, trying to make herself as small as possible, her terror-filled eyes wide. I came closer. Star's body blocked most of her victim from my view, so I couldn't tell which one of my guests she was trying to kill.

"I didn't do it," Tiffany whined. "I found Gabrella like this."

Well, that answered the who, but it didn't answer the what or the where. What was Bill's wife doing up here, and where was he?

"Run!" I shouted at Tiffany.

Tiffany, the survivor she is, hurtled past me toward the grand staircase almost before the word left my mouth.

"Aunt Laramie?" The voice came from an open doorway right beside the body Star was feasting on. Sheets missing, one of the twins stood in the opening. The other one knelt just inside the room with his arms latched around Bo, restraining her from attacking Star. Tears streamed down their faces.

Regret nearly overwhelmed me. I should have marched them up to the apartment and locked them in. They were little boys on Halloween. Of course they wouldn't go back to their mother when there was a party going on and a big house to explore.

"Get back in the room. Lock that door and don't open it

for anyone!" I yelled at them. "Now!" That did the trick. They dragged Bo back into the room and slammed the door.

I had to end this and get the boys to safety. I took stock of the situation, unsure how to proceed. If I body-slammed Star while she feasted, her fangs might rip open the victim's neck. Then I remembered Ora Lee's earlier move and sank my hands into the vampire's hair. I gave a quick tug, hoping Star would release the victim's neck, and then braced for a harder pull.

Yeah, that was a bad plan. You know the phrase 'grabbing the tiger by the tail?' Replace it with 'grabbing the vampire by the hair.' Star released the victim and turned on me. The next thing I knew, we were tumbling down the hall. When we came to a stop she was on top of me, hissing like a hellcat.

She drew back her fist to punch me, and I involuntarily closed my eyes. The punch never came. Van slammed into her and they rolled off me. I sprung to my feet. Damn, but she was some fighter, and agile to boot. She rolled once with Van, disengaged herself, gained her feet, and overtook Tiffany, who had just reached the grand staircase. I had to learn that trick.

In a single smooth movement, Star seized Tiffany and swung her around so they were facing us. Tiffany's head was clamped between her white hands.

"Take another step and I'll break her neck."

I froze. Van gained his feet and moved to stand between the vampire and me. He gasped for breath and his left arm hung at an unnatural angle. Somewhere during the tumble his cape had twisted, and a wide rip in his white shirtsleeve revealed a nasty gash that ran almost the length of his arm. In what seemed like slow motion, a drop of blood slid down one of his fingers and dripped onto the hardwood floor. With my entire being focused on it, I swear I heard the blood splash when it landed.

I spun to get the thought of Van's blood out of my mind and was confronted by the sight of Gabrella. Blood pooled like spilled merlot beneath her head, while matching red rivulets trickled from the fang holes in her neck. The overwhelming desire for blood washed over me. The warm, spicy scent of vanilla and cloves beckoned, and I dropped to my knees beside Gabrella's body.

13

THE CHASE

Van had once described vampires to me as "just things, little better than snakes or rabid dogs." Maybe he was right. At the very least, I was incompetent and weak. I hadn't been able to fight Star, and now I was unable to resist the lure of blood. I should just let Van take Star down. He was trained for this type of situation. I should just stay here with the body and—

"Laramie, no!" Van's yell brought me back to my senses, at least enough to take my eyes off the blood that oozed from the fang holes. With superhuman effort, I focused on Gabrella's face.

Its white pallor shocked me fully back into the events happening around me—the twins just a few feet away, Owen lying critically injured a floor below me, a vampire on the loose, and now Gabrella's blood pooling on the floor beneath her. Surely there was more blood than would come from a single bite.

Star's high-pitched laugh drew my attention and I stood and turned just in time to see her carrying Tiffany up the grand staircase toward the third floor. Van was in the hallway between us, obviously undecided about who needed saving the most—Tiffany from Star, or Gabrella from me.

Daisy was on the third floor. I would have to leave Gabrella. The boys could stay in the room for a little while longer; I trusted Bo to take care of them. With a burst of speed, I passed Van and headed after Star.

I mentally reviewed the top floor as I ran. The grand staircase opened onto a long hallway that ran the length of the floor. Long ago, Hattie had combined several small servants' rooms that took up the entire right side of the third floor into a suite for herself. I had taken that over, and that's where Daisy was now. The rear staircase opened directly into my suite, so Star couldn't escape down those stairs unless she went through my apartment. I always kept its main door locked. I sent an urgent prayer up to the gods: Please don't let Daisy wander into the hallway to check out the ruckus.

Hattie had left the other side of the third floor in its original form, with small rooms opening into the long hallway. I had locked all the doors on that side earlier this evening too, in case any of the guests disregarded the ropes.

As long as Daisy stayed locked in my apartment, I had Star trapped.

I briefly considered the steps that led from the third floor up to the widow's walk that topped my house. Heights terrified me, and I'd only been up there once with Bill, to discuss its restoration. I referred to it as the Platform of Death, or POD for short. Bill's crew had replaced the railing around the walk and installed architectural lighting so it would look nice from the street. I hadn't even gone up to inspect the work. The staircase, little more than a ladder, was in one of the tiny rooms off the third-floor hallway. Before the party I had double-checked that the door was locked, as I didn't want any guests to end up on my roof. The lock wouldn't hold up against a vampire, but there was no way Star could even know which door led to the roof.

Except that's where she was standing when I reached the third floor, almost as if I had willed it to be so. Her arm was hooked around Tiffany's neck. This night kept getting worse and worse. Why was it so hard to keep doors in The Madam locked?

Star hissed at me and dragged Tiffany through the open doorway. I had to give Tiffany credit. She hadn't fainted at the sight of two vampires fighting, or at being held hostage by one. She grabbed the doorframe and hung on for dear life. Tiffany was a fighter, but she didn't have the vampire's strength. Star half-carried, half-dragged her up the rough wooden steps to the roof and shoved open the trapdoor.

"Ow! Stop it! I'm caught!" Tiffany screamed.

I entered the small room just as Tiffany's feet disappeared through the opening. The trapdoor banged shut. Crimson smeared a splintered step and the door's gray wooden frame. Tiffany must have been gouged by the jagged plank and was now leaving a trail of blood.

I tried not to inhale its scent. I didn't want Tiffany's blood on my hands, or fangs, or whatever, if I couldn't control myself when the bloodlust took over. Despite my efforts, its odor still reached me, but it smelled odd. It wasn't fragrant. It was even a little off-putting. What was it? Something salty or fishy? Whatever it was, it didn't affect me the way the other blood had.

I stopped midway up the ladder. I told myself it was to process the odor, but the real reason was that I didn't want to go up on that roof. Then, unable to stop myself, I touched a smear of Tiffany's blood and brought my finger to my mouth. Ugh! It was awful.

Van's footsteps pounding down the hallway galvanized me into action. I didn't want him to see me acting so cowardly when someone's life was at stake, even if she was a nasty piece of work. I took another step upward and placed my hand against the trapdoor.

Just push it open, Laramie. You can do this, I told myself. It's not like a fall off the roof will kill you. It won't even hurt you. Much.

Tiffany's high-pitched scream, so loud that it traveled through the trapdoor, got me moving again. I shoved the door. As it flew upwards I pushed off the ladder, propelling myself through the opening and onto The Madam's widow's walk.

14

THE PLATFORM OF DEATH

The widow's walk is a rectangular platform that sits atop The Madam's roof at its highest peak. It's about twenty feet long and fifteen feet wide. A wooden picket railing surrounds the structure at hip level, but it's more ornamental than practical.

Widow's walks have graced the roofs of houses for centuries, built so the wives of ship captains could watch for their husbands' return. Since vessels were often lost at sea, many of the women who walked the platforms were widows long before they knew it. That a widow's walk topped The Madam, in the middle of landlocked Dallas, was a testament to how pretentious—or crazy—Jad's family had been for over a century. There wasn't even a view of nearby Turtle Creek from up here, much less an ocean.

Star was at the farthest end of the platform from the trapdoor, holding Tiffany in a tight embrace and drinking deeply from her neck. Van's condemnation of vampires came back to me for the second time that night. She *was* little more than a rabid thing. But with the way I was reacting to the smallest smear of blood myself, was I any better? Maybe taking us both over the edge wouldn't be such a bad thing. If one of The Madam's many wooden embellishments impaled us on the way down, wouldn't I be doing the world a favor?

I shook my head to dislodge the image. I wasn't ready to call it quits just yet, but the macabre thought gave me an idea. Sending my silent regrets to Bill for destroying his crew's beautiful work, I pulled one of the wooden pickets loose from the railing and broke it over my knee. I examined the impromptu stake, hoping the jagged break was pointy enough.

Star's eyes grew wide and she pushed Tiffany away from her. I savored my moment of triumph. I had finally struck fear into someone tonight, and I was going to enjoy my badass moment.

"You aren't human!" Star screeched.

Well, duh. I thought she had clicked on that when we were fighting—okay, when she was kicking my butt—in the saloon. I extended my fangs, just in case she'd missed them.

But she hadn't been talking to me.

"Am too!" Tiffany shot back, looking insulted.

"You aren't," Star insisted. "The blood will tell."

What was she talking about? But Van was coming through the trapdoor's opening, so I didn't wait to find out. I ran toward the vampire, the stake held high. Star anticipated me and picked up Tiffany as if she were little more than a rag doll, then threw her at me.

The move caught me off guard. I dropped the stake and caught Tiffany mid-air. With her in my arms, I was assaulted by the odor of the blood pouring from a gash in her shoulder and the fang holes in her neck. I say assaulted because it wasn't appealing at all. The fishy stench made me want to toss her away from me.

"Laramie!" Van yelled.

I looked up to see Star standing on the railing that surrounded the widow's walk, getting ready to take him down.

She reminded me of those WWF wrestlers Jad had loved to watch, who stood on the ropes before launching themselves onto their opponents in the ring.

I unceremoniously dumped Tiffany onto the plank flooring, trying to ignore a surge of satisfaction from her low "whoof" when she landed. I charged forward, placing myself between Van and Star. Blood covered the arm that hung uselessly by his side, but I used every ounce of willpower I possessed to block its aroma and focus on protecting him from her attack.

Star's muscles bunched as she prepared to leap. They were easy to see because her minuscule red dress barely covered her private bits, much less anything else. Somewhere during the run through The Madam, she'd lost her strappy stilettos. Her gaze stayed riveted on Van.

I crouched, lowering my center of gravity like a goalie preparing to block a shot. She would not get to him.

A whirring noise caught me by surprise, and I just made out a silver knife as it flew past me. I glanced back at Van and saw him pulling a second knife from his cloak. The Van Helsing siblings deserved expert marks for their ability to hide weapons in Halloween costumes. I turned back just in time to see Star stop the first knife mid-air by trapping it between her hands, its tip mere inches from her chest.

She screamed as smoke billowed from her hands. The knife was genuine silver, or at least silver-plated. The metal, one of the few substances that can truly hurt vampires, burns our skin at the slightest touch. She paused only a moment before gripping the handle and lobbing it back at Van. She didn't have his knife-throwing skills, but she had vampire strength behind her fling. Without thinking, I threw my body between the knife and Van, twisting at the last moment to protect my chest.

"No!" Van yelled, and an instant before the knife hit me, I

heard the whir of his second blade. Then Star's throw pierced my upper shoulder. The silver blade passed unhindered through skin and muscle and embedded itself in the bone, sending a painful shock wave throughout my body. The force of its impact had me rolling across the widow's walk.

Star's shriek rent the night. I glimpsed her standing on the top rail, windmilling her arms, fighting for balance. Van's second knife protruded from her torso. Unable to recover, she toppled backward off the banister.

I pushed to my feet and stumbled to the railing in a haze of pain. The vampire rested a few feet below the widow's walk, in a valley made by two of the roof's peaks. I watched her pull the silver knife from her chest, gasping. The effort cost her the grip she tenaciously held on The Madam's wet slates. She slipped a few feet closer to the edge of the roof.

I've only seen one vampire die. The wooden stake I had driven into her chest impaled her heart, and within seconds, fiery cracks and crevices covered her skin. Then she combusted and turned into a pile of ash.

But Star's skin—and she was showing a lot of it—was still a beautiful, glowing white, as smooth as porcelain. There was nary a fiery fissure in sight. Van must have missed her heart. But the silver had done its number on her, just as it was doing on me. She appeared weak and a little disoriented.

"Hold on, I'm coming!" I called.

I straddled the railing. Then with one foot inside the relative safety of the widow's walk and the other on the unprotected edge of the platform, I realized what I was doing and froze. Not because I was trying to save a homicidal vampire; I no longer cared that Star had tried to kill me and several of my guests. She was in distress and needed my help. No, the problem was that I was three stories up and about to go out onto a slate roof covered in the slick sheen of an October night's mist, with a silver knife embedded in my shoulder, leeching my strength.

Star lay several feet below me, her grip on the damp slates the only thing between safety and a long fall. Her eyes met mine, but instead of the hate I had seen projected each time she attacked me, they were large and sad.

"Why doesn't he want me?" she said.

"Who?" But a part of me already knew.

"He made us. He wants you and the other one. Why didn't Jad want me, too?" Star released her grip on the slate and slid toward the edge. Her eyes held mine until she disappeared into the darkness like a person descending into a still, black pool.

"Laramie, get back!" Van, tugged on my good arm, trying to urge me back to the safety of the widow's walk.

Reason reasserted itself. I swung my leg back over the rail, but a dark wave washed over me, probably caused by the silver in my system. I fell backwards over the railing. The long, flowing sleeve of my dress tore and I slid free of it, leaving Van holding a scrap of material.

I somehow caught the edge of the deck with the hand of my uninjured arm and clung for dear life.

"Laramie, I've got you." Van grabbed my wrist through the pickets.

I felt the railing shift against his weight. "Van, let go! If the railing gives way, the fall will kill you. I'll survive, remember?"

"Come on, get your feet under you and climb over," he commanded, ignoring my order.

"Van Helsing Anderson, if you don't get off this roof right this minute, I swear I'll let go." I meant it, too. I couldn't live if Van died trying to save me.

"For God's sake, Laramie, I'm not letting go!"

"Yeah, quit being such a drama queen and get your ass back on this side of the railing." Tiffany, bloody and battered, stood next to him. Who knew she had it in her to help anyone but herself?

I climbed over the railing drunkenly, and a bit huffily, I

might add, then turned to scan the grounds of The Madam for Star.

The vampire had vanished.

15

BAD TO THE BONE

Bunny arrived as Van was helping me down through the trapdoor. Although his left arm hung uselessly by his side, he was the stronger of the two of us at that moment. I was dizzy with relief at being off the roof. Or maybe it was the effect of the silver blade still embedded in my shoulder.

Tiffany and Van's wounds had clotted, but they still reeked of blood. The scent of Van's blood—earthy, with hints of leather and smoke—was alluring, but I was too weak to attack. Tiffany left us as soon as she got inside, heading for the grand staircase at a fast clip. She would probably run all the way to the front door. Good riddance.

"Get the knife out," I whispered. "Silver." Its tip had lodged in the bone and pain radiated through my body. It had already seared the surrounding flesh like a hot poker, though the wound no longer smoked.

"Should we sit her down?" Bunny asked.

"No, I've got her." Van wrapped his good arm tightly around me and nodded at her.

Bunny grabbed the knife's hilt, braced herself, and pulled. It didn't budge.

"I'll get Grace or Marek. It will take their strength to get it out."

"You know them?" I asked weakly. The edges of my vision were darkening, but I still caught the look they shared.

"I've had the pleasure of meeting them a few times over the years, and they're downstairs now. They arrived just in time to help LaRue contain your guests. I don't know how much longer her ritual would have held."

"I bet Grace was pissed she missed out on the action." My knees gave way. If Van hadn't been holding me, I would have dropped to the floor.

"Yeah, she said something to that effect, but in a lot more colorful terminology," Bunny said. "At least I believe it was. I need to brush up on my Irish. Anyway, they're downstairs now, *convincing* the guests that the fight was all a Halloween show put on for their benefit."

Van groaned.

I assumed, from the stress Bunny put on the word 'convincing' and Van's reaction, that they doubted Marek and Grace's powers of persuasion. I didn't blame them. The performance angle was a great idea in theory, but it would take more than Grace and Marek's salesmanship abilities to make people forget what they'd seen with their own eyes. Still, a girl could hope.

I tried to cross my fingers and hope that they could salvage my reputation, but my fingers wouldn't work.

"Hurry up, Bunny," Van said. "The silver is already affecting her coordination."

Bunny turned to head downstairs.

"Owen . . ." I mumbled.

She turned back. "He's going to be okay. So is the woman on the second floor. Ora Lee administered some of her vamp blood to Owen and he perked right up. Then as we were heading up here to help you out with Star, Ora Lee locked on to the scent of her victim's blood. Luckily, we got to her in time.

In addition to the vampire bite, she had a serious wound to the back of her head and had lost a lot of blood. When she came to, she told us her name was Gabrella and asked for her husband. I think she said his name was Bill, but we haven't had time to search for him."

I managed a slight nod to signal my relief. Vampire blood cures almost anything, if it's administered in time. I squelched a twinge of jealousy over Ora Lee's ability to resist the lure of blood.

I felt, more than saw, Van wave at Bunny to hurry.

She turned and ran down the hall faster than humanly possible, the cotton tail on her costume bouncing merrily. Despite her enhanced abilities, before tonight I had never seen Bunny move at a pace faster than would be socially acceptable for a lady of leisure.

Van lowered me so I was sitting with my back propped against the wall, and then joined me on the floor. Even in my fuzzy condition, I could feel the pain radiating off him. The gash that ran the length of his arm had to smart, and from the way his arm hung, I'd bet a bottle of wine his shoulder was dislocated.

"Blood?" I held up my skewered arm to him. "Heal faster."

His face contorted in disgust before he could conceal his reaction. "Uh, no, I'm a pretty fast healer on my own."

"Suit yourself." No sooner had I closed my eyes than a breeze blew over me. Someone needed to close the trapdoor to the widow's walk.

"That was quick," Van said.

"I was upstairs helping with the injured woman and the other situation." The breeze was from Marek's arrival. "A knife in the arm shouldn't be causing her this much trouble."

What other situation? I thought fuzzily, but couldn't form the words.

"It's silver," Van explained. "Here, wrap my cape around the hilt so you don't burn yourself."

Marek braced me with one arm and, using Van's cape like a glove, gripped the knife. "Laramie, this may cause you some pain."

But it didn't. Not even a little. The burning agony miraculously disappeared and my flesh began to knit back together.

"Dislocated shoulder? I can move that back into place for you," Marek said, I presumed to Van. Although the pain had receded, I was still too weak to open my eyes.

"It's fine. Bunny can fix it for me or I will see a doctor. We need to get downstairs."

Marek sighed. "Why must the Van Helsings, you in particular, always make everything so difficult?"

"Don't touch me! I said don't!"

My eyes snapped open. Marek held Van effortlessly, one hand on his good shoulder and the other on his injured arm.

Crack!

"Mother Fu—!" Van yelled as his shoulder popped back into its socket.

Then he was striding up and down the hallway, rolling his shoulder and shaking his previously dislocated arm. Marek retreated to the end of the hallway and leaned against the wall, waiting to see if we needed more help.

"He's a hottie, isn't he?" Bunny asked, dropping to the floor beside me.

"Your brother?" I asked.

"Ew! No, Marek." She whispered. Marek's slight grimace alerted me that with his supernatural hearing, he was following our conversation. "Imagine the skills he's picked up over the centuries. It makes my pulse race just thinking about it." Bunny fanned herself. I peeked again at the vampire.

Marek wore his customary black from head to toe. No Halloween costume for him. I didn't blame him. The dark clothing complemented the flowing, midnight-black hair that just brushed his shoulders. His pale skin and chiseled features contributed to a mysterious and intriguing appeal. He appeared to be in his early thirties. I was unsure of his exact age, but I knew that he counted it in centuries rather than years.

I did a double take. His grimace had turned into a bemused smile. So Bunny affected him the same way she did the rest of us. I liked it. That she threw him off kilter somehow made him more normal.

Somewhere in The Madam a dog barked, triggering a memory and shattering the moment.

"The twins!" I exclaimed.

16

TRUST ISSUES

"The twins!" I repeated and tried to stand. Van sped back to us. As he and Bunny helped me to my feet, I tried to tell him about Daisy and the twins.

Bunny interrupted me. "Laramie, they're okay. Owen got them to open the door and Marek, uh, calmed them down. Owen has taken them upstairs to their mother. Also, Gabrella remembers nothing about the attack, so that is a plus."

I sagged with relief, then buried my face in Van's Dracula cape. The boys were unharmed, and Gabrella didn't remember the vampire. That was good news to me. But when I explained, still leaning on Van, about my sister-in-law and the boys' arrival and my promise to keep their presence a secret, he tensed and drew away. I reluctantly released him. It felt so good to lean on someone—literally and figuratively.

"So Monty doesn't know his wife and children are here?" Van asked, switching seamlessly into his 'just the facts' cop voice.

"No, he was here earlier, but I didn't tell him. He may still be downstairs with the rest of the family." The thought of facing them filled me with dread. How was I going to explain Star's attack on Cheyenne?

"No," Bunny broke in. "After Grace talked to people, she asked them to leave. I think she started with Cheyenne and your mother because they were so upset."

The favors I owed Grace kept piling up. I would have to face the music at some point with my family, but at least it wouldn't be tonight.

"And the woman who was injured—Gabrella? Who is she, and what was she doing here tonight?" Van asked.

"She and her husband own the company that renovated The Madam. Remember, her husband Bill was the contractor."

"Ah, and Tiffany was Bill's mistress?" Van asked. When I nodded, he rolled his eyes and said, "I'd better go double-check on Gabrella. As long as Daisy is okay and the boys are with her, that situation can wait until tomorrow. Stay here, okay?"

I nodded, and inwardly I sighed with relief. Van and my brother were good friends, and it wouldn't have surprised me if he'd insisted on calling Monty right that minute.

Bunny waited until Van and Marek were out of earshot, then she whispered, "Jad left. When we ran out of the storeroom after Star crash-landed in the saloon, I glanced back and saw him headed out the rear door. He had the cheek to salute me. While we were all running toward the fight, he took his opportunity to escape."

"Bastard," I responded.

"Rat bastard."

"Bunny, I would never—"

"I know," she interrupted. "Laramie, I see the way you look at my brother. You were taken in by Jad's costume. If only I had told you what Van's costume was, you wouldn't have confused the two."

"Bunny, no. It's not your fault. Jad always liked to stir things up. I practically threw myself at him, and he couldn't resist having a little fun. But I wonder what he was doing here?"

"Up to no good, is what. A Halloween party was the perfect chance for him to get in and out of The Madam unrecognized. You need to do an inventory of the Van Helsing-Harper Annex as soon as possible." At my huff, she rolled her eyes. "Fine, The Bat Cave, but it doesn't have the same ring. Ask Van for an inventory of what he and Jad brought over from The Compound. Better yet, Owen and I will be happy to do it for you."

"Thanks, Bunny. Do you think Van will believe me . . . about the kiss?"

She glanced hurriedly down the hallway. Van was returning to join us.

"Laramie, he looks at you the same way you look at him. But . . . It's hard for him, being the Van Helsing heir. Van's always had to carry that weight," she whispered urgently. "Oh, and I told Grace and Marek about the kiss so there won't be awkward questions later."

Then Van was back. "Where are you going?" he asked Bunny when she sashayed to the stairs.

"I'm going to go see what I can find out about Ora Lee. Stay with Laramie, she needs you now." Bunny gave me a conspiratorial wink and lightly skipped down the stairs, the fluffy white poof bouncing at each step.

Van told me that Gabrella was doing well, all things considered. She was sitting up, and Star's bite had completely disappeared. A gaping head wound responsible for the majority of the bleeding was now little more than a scratch. But she couldn't remember anything about the attack. Tiffany, who had joined the group looking after Gabrella, wasn't taking it well. He said that she kept murmuring, "I didn't do it."

I figured the less anyone at this party recalled about vampire attacks, bites, and fights, the better. Without Star,

Tiffany was the main suspect. She probably wanted Gabrella to remember the bloodthirsty assault.

Van steered me toward the stairs, his arm holding me tenderly against his side. I hated to ruin the moment, but I had to clear up what happened downstairs.

"Van, about Jad—"

"Have you been hiding him here?"

"What? No!"

He frowned. "That vampire, Star, seemed to think you were."

"You believe that I would allow him into my house? Let him stay here?"

Van's jaw tensed, but his words came out low and even, "No. It's just when she said it, she seemed so certain. And you were kissing him."

"I was not! Okay, I was, but I didn't realize he was Jad." I wasn't explaining this correctly, but he had thrown me for a loop with the hiding Jad accusation.

"It's okay Laramie, I know it wasn't your fault."

"Thank God, Van. I'm glad you realize I would never knowingly kiss Jad."

We stopped on the second floor. Van turned to me, but gazed at a point just over my shoulder. "Laramie, I don't hold you responsible for that kiss. I understand that you can't control the heightened emotions and, well, urges you are experiencing as a vampire. The residual feelings you have for Jad overcame you. After we find the True Cross and turn you back into my Laramie, I'll never have to worry about anything like that happening again."

"Wait, what?" I asked, dumbfounded. "I didn't know it was Jad. I thought he was you. Because of his costume."

"Look, what happened here tonight wasn't your fault, so please don't lie to me about it. You are a vampire. I can't expect you to control your lust—or to resist blood, for that matter. I realize that I just have to accept you for what you are until we can change you back."

Van smiled down at me and smoothed an errant lock of hair behind my ear. Then, thoroughly convinced of his rightness and my gratefulness, he waited for me to swoon.

But I was seeing pink. "What I am? Am I really just a thing to you? You saw how hard I worked tonight, on this party, on keeping my friends and family safe. Is that how—"

"Laramie!" Bill Martinez, looking dazed, moved up the grand staircase toward us.

I glanced back up at Van. His face was set in hard lines, and I couldn't read his response to my angry questions. I would be a hypocrite not to admit, at least to myself, that I had thought the same thing earlier about my reaction to blood. But Van had practically called me a liar. Could I be with someone who didn't trust my word, no matter how much I loved him? Or, worse, someone who saw only a creature when he looked at me?

"Hey Bill," I responded shakily when he joined us at the top of the stairs.

"Have you seen Gabrella? She was with me when the show started, but I can't seem to find her now."

I paused, uncertain of what show he was talking about. Then I remembered Bunny saying that Marek and Grace had convinced the partygoers the vampire fight was a performance. But hadn't Gabrella been upstairs when Star attacked her?

"Bill, she is up here. She had an accident, but she is going to be fine." I pointed down the hallway.

Bill spotted Gabrella sitting in the hallway talking to Marek and hurried to her.

Owen left Gabrella's side to make room for Bill and then joined Van and me, followed by Bo, Dixie, and Buck.

"The boys are fine," Owen assured me before I could ask.

"And Daisy?"

"She is sound asleep in your room."

"I should go check on her," I told Van, thankful for the opportunity to put some distance between us until I came to grips with what he had said.

"You don't need to. Plus, it will mean walking past the crime scene," Owen said with a smile. But he didn't fool me. He had heard how much trouble I'd had dealing with blood tonight. Boy, bad news travels fast.

I couldn't deny that he had a point. The safest place for me, and the humans, was downstairs. I opened my mouth to say as much to Owen, but then I noticed the tattered, blood-covered state of his leprechaun costume. Somewhere along the way he had lost the ridiculous top hat and his hair stood on end.

"How are you doing?" I began choking up, but forced out, "I was scared I was going to lose you."

"Ora Lee saved me. I'm barely sore." Owen's forehead creased. "Everything is so surreal."

Being careful to avoid the blood, I squeezed his arm. I didn't have to say anything. Owen recognized that I understood exactly how it felt to have a loved one come back from the dead.

MIND GAMES

Van helped me down the stairs, with Bo, Dixie, and Buck at our heels. All three dogs must have been in the room with the twins. I sent up a silent thank you to the gods that they, along with the boys, were unscathed.

Don and Cheryl waited at the bottom of the grand staircase. The saloon was otherwise empty of guests. Grace was there, starting to clean up.

"There's our boy!" Don swept Buck up into his arms.

"We loved the show, Laramie. It was so realistic! I'll call you about Don's party," Cheryl called over her shoulder as they left.

At least two people had fallen for the 'story,' which gave me hope that the rest might have, too.

I scanned the room. Luckily, the damage from the fight was minimal. Grace, a stunningly beautiful centuries-old vampire who had been a pirate queen during her human years, was setting tables and chairs back into place. She was surprisingly domestic when circumstances called for it. She, like Marek, had forgone a costume for the festivities.

"Where'd everybody go?" I asked.

"Marek flew to your aid at Miss Anderson, eh, Bunny's,

request. LaRue is combing the grounds for any trace of the visiting vampires. And wouldn't it be best to send all on their way after we compelled them?" Grace asked in her beautiful Irish lilt, as if compelling people was the most natural thing in the world. Perhaps it was for her, but I didn't understand what she meant. Then Bunny's references to "convincing" and "helping" fell into place.

"Mind control? Why? How?" I sat down heavily on a nearby chair.

Grace stopped righting chairs and tossed her flowing red hair back over her shoulders. It was her go-to move when exasperated. Thankfully, I wasn't the object of her ire.

"We have failed in our duty to you," she said. "That ends tomorrow. Marek and I will begin your training." Then, realizing that she hadn't answered my question, she continued, "Compelling exchanges an original memory or thought with a created one. That is what we did to your friends tonight. We compelled them to believe that what they had seen was not a vicious fight involving vampires, but rather a staged performance of people in vampire costumes to entertain them. But playing with a human mind, or that of another vampire, is a tenuous thing. We plant an idea in the person's consciousness, but their unconscious is always trying to override the falseness of the compelled version with the truth of the real one. The longer people were to remain together and talk about the evening, the more the truth would try to break free. Whereas if they go on their way quickly, their mind moves on to other things and the compelled memory or idea will less likely be challenged and is more likely to hold."

Surprisingly, I understood exactly what she meant. It was a tantalizing concept. Could I change Van's memory of the kiss with Jad to something less innocuous? *Stop it, Laramie!* Grace had just said it was a tenuous thing to play with someone's mind. Besides, shouldn't Van trust me without my having to resort to mind control?

While Grace explained, Van stood beside my chair. But the fragrance of the blood that still clung to him was intoxicating, so I stood up and walked away. Someone had cleaned up the pool of Owen's blood. Unfortunately, its odor still lingered, its coppery scent mixing with Van's earthier tones.

"Star, one of the vampires who crashed the party, said that Jad made her, too," I told Grace, more to distract myself from the blood than anything else. I expected her to be shocked and turn the air blue with cursing, but she only walked to the bar and poured three glasses of red wine.

"We should wait for the others so we can share information," she said, selecting the table farthest from where Owen's blood had been spilled and indicating that Van and I join her. "We have learned much over the last few days."

That was an understatement. Between Jad showing up at The Madam, me kissing him, more vampires than we could shake a stick at—one of them Owen's presumed dead sister—fighting it out in front of all my guests, and the attack on Gabrella, it might take all night to catch everyone up to speed.

I knew Grace wanted me to wait, but I couldn't help adding one more thing—more of a question, really. "Star was so much stronger than me."

"Because she drinks blood." Grace sighed. "Isn't it how we are built? When we abstain, we grow weaker. I know you don't want to drink blood, love. But if we must fight others of our kind, you will have to."

"No!" Van said. "She barely controlled herself tonight. She nearly attacked two people. We don't want to give her the taste for blood."

"We all have the taste for blood. It's what we are. Did you bite anyone?" Grace asked me.

"No," I murmured and then felt I should add, "But it was a close thing." I gulped my wine.

"That is excellent," Grace said. "You did well to resist when there was so much spilled tonight. I have had centuries to learn to control the bloodlust, but even I'm busying myself to take my mind off the scents that permeate the house. That you overcame it, no matter how near a thing it was, is an achievement."

I felt a warm glow suffuse me. Grace didn't give compliments willy-nilly. I had wanted to show Van tonight that I could handle being a vampire. Although it hadn't gone exactly to plan, surely after hearing Grace's praise he would realize that it hadn't been a total disaster.

But when I looked at him, he refused to meet my gaze. Had Grace's words meant nothing to him?

I turned back to her. "I don't know how much you know about what went on upstairs. But we also have to find out what happened to Gabrella. My guess is that her head injury happened during the vampire attack, though Tiffany is acting awfully hinky."

"Who are Gabrella and Tiffany?" Grace asked.

That was my first inkling that our problems extended beyond vampires and ex-husbands. My next one came a second later when Marek, gripping her arm tightly, escorted Tiffany down the staircase. Bunny followed close behind, worry forming a deep line between her eyebrows.

"We have a situation," Marek said grimly.

18

THE SIREN'S SONG

Boy, did we ever have a situation. As previously mentioned, we had several situations.

"She isn't human. I am unable to compel her," Marek said flatly when he and Tiffany stopped in front of us.

Star's words on the widow's walk came back to me. The blood will tell. Was that why I was able to resist Tiffany's blood; why it was unappealing?

"And what would you be?" Grace asked, cutting to the chase.

"I'm a human," Tiffany argued. "Just what the hell are y'all?"

Grace wasn't the only straight shooter here.

"Star said you weren't human," I pointed out. "I bet you attacked Gabrella. Come clean right now or we'll call the police."

Grace cleared her throat and widened her eyes at me in the universal 'shut the hell up' look.

"Oh, give me a break. You won't be calling the police. You have more to hide than I do," Tiffany shot back. "And I didn't attack the bitch."

"Then what were you doing upstairs with her?" Van asked, going all Columbo on her.

"And where is Mateo? Remember him, the guy you came with?" I threw in for good measure.

"Mateo left the party. He disappeared right after we arrived and then texted me he was leaving. I went upstairs looking for Bill after *she*," Tiffany jerked her head in my direction, but somehow held on to the wide-eyed innocent look she was directing at Van, "ran him out of the kitchen." Tiffany paused, but Van waved impatiently for her to continue. When she saw he wasn't buying the act, her face hardened and she turned to me.

"It was obvious Bill didn't want you to see us together. So as soon as you disappeared into the storeroom, I slid past those two cute cowboys who followed you and headed up the back stairs to the second floor. It was dark, and I tripped over Gabrella. She was unconscious and bleeding. Before I could say boo, the slutty chick was running toward us. When she reached us, it was like she hit a brick wall. Then she just dropped and latched onto Gabrella's neck."

Van gave me a long look followed by a light shrug of his good shoulder. I assumed that he thought Tiffany was omitting chunks of her story, as did I. But he was leaving it up to me whether to pursue it.

"So no one can account for where you were between the time you were talking to Bill and when his wife was attacked. And you're telling us that Gabrella was already unconscious before the vamp . . . before Star attacked her." I couldn't let it go.

"I didn't do it," Tiffany insisted. "The slutty chick must have attacked her before I found her and then returned to finish her off."

I thought she protested a little too much, but there was no proof that she had attacked Gabrella before Star did, even if that was what happened. I was clutching at straws. A bloodthirsty vampire had been on the loose in my house and I was trying to pin an attack on Tiffany simply because I didn't like her. That didn't show me in the best light.

The sound of steps on my grand staircase pulled me from my contemplations on Tiffany's viability as an attempted murderess. Bill and Gabrella descended the stairs, arms wrapped around each other, Owen a few steps behind.

"She doesn't remember who, if anyone, attacked her," Marek confided to me in a low voice. "When she regained consciousness, her belief was that she had fallen and hit her head. I compelled them that they were happy and had an exquisite time at your party. I let the belief that she fell and bumped her head stand. This isn't our problem and we need to stay out of it."

Seeing Bill reminded me that no one knew where he had been when Gabrella was attacked. Marek had spoken almost as if he'd read my mind. Who knew, perhaps he had. That was something I needed to learn about, too.

I opened my mouth to point out that someone getting attacked in The Madam was definitely my business, but Bill, Gabrella, and Owen joined us so I closed it again.

"Where is Ora Lee?" Bunny asked them.

Our gazes swung to the trio.

"Who?" Bill and Gabrella asked at the same time.

"Ora Lee?" Owen asked. "My sister is dead. Wait, how do you know Ora Lee?"

He looked at us in confusion. A tremor shook his body, then he swung around to stare up the stairs. He turned back to us, his face contorted. "Was Ora Lee here? But how?"

"I'm not sure who y'all are talking about, but I need to get Gabrella home," Bill said, holding his wife close to his side in a careful embrace.

"I am tired," Gabrella agreed. She smiled lovingly up into his face.

Tiffany's low retching noises ruined the moment, but Bill

and Gabrella didn't notice. They only had eyes and ears for each other.

No one spoke for several moments after they left The Madam.

"Ora Lee compelled all three of them to forget she was ever here," Bunny said, admiration clear in her voice.

Crap! Was I the only vampire in the world who didn't know how to compel people?

I noticed LaRue standing quietly by the swinging door into the kitchen. Her face was tight and pinched. It wasn't like LaRue to hold back.

"I don't understand—" Owen started, but Grace cut him off.

"We have much to discuss, but this one must be dealt with first." She nodded at Tiffany.

"Hey, I am not someone 'to be dealt with.' I know things about you. About all of you." Tiffany waved her hand to encompass our entire group. "Things you don't want floating around Dallas."

"And what would herself be wanting?" Grace asked.

"I want a job," Tiffany replied, crossing her arms. At our blank looks, she added, "Here. I can start immediately."

"No way!" I protested.

"Agreed," Grace replied, cutting over my refusal. Then she spoke to me. "When shall she begin?"

"Can't we just kill her?" I was only partly kidding. Grace raised an eyebrow at me.

"Fine. Come by tomorrow at five, and I'll get you started on the paperwork and training," I said huffily. What good was all this vampire stuff if I could get pushed around, not to mention blackmailed, this easily?

"See you tomorrow. Boss," Tiffany sneered, then walked out the front door without bothering to close it behind her.

"Succubus?" Van asked LaRue.

"Possibly, but there is something else there, too," LaRue responded tersely.

"Siren. The fish stench coming off her was dead rotten," Grace said.

"That makes more sense," LaRue agreed. Then she realized that she had agreed with Grace, a vampire, and added sulkily, "I would have known that if I had your sense of smell."

"Ah love, sure you would have," Grace replied easily. "And couldn't she be part succubus, too? Either would explain how she acts around men; and a pairing of the two? Well, that would make clear a lot of her other shortcomings, too."

"Her blood tasted like rotten fish," I added hesitantly.

Van and LaRue both cringed, but Grace murmured, "Ah, yes. The blood will tell."

"That's what Star said," I agreed. "Isn't a siren a mermaid?"

"Eh," Van, LaRue, and Grace all replied with shrugs that indicated maybe, but not exactly, and still didn't clear up what the hell Tiffany was.

"Okay, let's table that for now, but will you answer me why I should let her work here? She already knows too much about us, and now she'll be here all the time. Couldn't you have given her a job at the Dragonfly? You have a lot more employees and can stick her somewhere out of the way. I don't have that luxury."

Grace rounded on me. "We will teach you how to vampire, and you have our protection until you get your legs about you, because that is what's right. But Tiffany is your problem, and, therefore, yours to deal with. We would do you a disservice if we handled the situation any other way."

Marek, who in typical Marek fashion had remained mostly silent, now spoke. "Tiffany is a supernatural. I find it an improbable coincidence that she started affairs with two men who could bring her into your house. We must watch her.

Keep your friends close and your enemies closer." He murmured the last part to himself, but I heard it. His Slavic accent gave the adage a sinister connotation.

"Marek, you've lived this long by being suspicious of everyone and everything, but this is paranoid, even for you," Van said, mirroring my thoughts exactly. "Tiffany and Bill's relationship probably began before he started work on The Madam."

"It didn't. I checked," Marek responded. "Grace and I have checked on a lot of things over the last two weeks. That brings us to our next issue."

Marek walked to the staircase and crouched on his haunches. During our conversation, Owen had sat on the bottom step. He gazed into Marek's eyes and then into mine. Resignation and regret etched his face in sad lines.

"Tell us how you came to work for Laramie, and why," Marek ordered Owen.

19

BETRAYED

Before Owen could answer, Grace suggested that we move the conversation to a larger table. She gathered clean glasses and several bottles of wine left over from the party and brought them over. I sank numbly into a chair and, hostess duties be damned, pushed my now-empty glass in front of her so it was the first glass she filled. I emptied it in two gulps and motioned for her to refill it. Van sat next to me, LaRue beside him. Bunny settled in the chair closest to Owen. No one suggested she leave. Despite her staking Owen, she had proven herself worthy to be a part of the group tonight. Finally, Bo and Dixie settled themselves underneath, no doubt hoping for dropped tidbits from the party.

I prayed that Owen hadn't had an ulterior motive in coming to work for me or in developing our friendship. He was my only true friend right now. The only one who accepted me for exactly who I was and who would support me in becoming my best self, whether it be vampire or human. I couldn't lose that.

When we were settled, Marek nodded at Owen.

"The paranormal always interested Ora Lee. Even before she got sick." Owen looked at me. "When we were in our early twenties, she developed ovarian cancer. She had a hysterectomy and went through chemo. For a while there, it was touch and go."

Owen and I had talked about his sister several times over the last two weeks, but he hadn't told me about the cancer. All I knew was that she'd killed herself two years ago, after Bernie Wallach (yes, the same Bernie who was murdered in The Madam) caused her bookshop and coffee house to go bankrupt. She sold books with a paranormal, occult bent—witchcraft, voodoo, ghosts, that type of thing—in her shop The Bewitched Bean.

Owen ran a hand through his hair. "After she recovered she became obsessed with the occult, religion, and vampires. She read everything she could get her hands on about eternal life, whether it be religious afterlife or immortality. When our parents died, she took her portion of the inheritance and opened the bookshop. I assumed it was a way for her to meet people who were searching for the same things she was."

"What does this have to do with why you are working for Laramie?" Van asked coldly.

"Van, please let him tell it in his own time," I murmured. Van was angry at himself because he hadn't checked Tiffany's story, much less Owen's, but I didn't want him to take it out on my friend.

Van sat back in his chair with his arms crossed. I placed my hand on his shoulder, but kept my focus on Owen.

"Laramie, it's okay. I want it all out in the open," Owen said. "I knew the shop was in trouble, but not the extent. I also failed to realize how depressed Ora Lee was . . ." He gave himself a slight shake and then continued. "She took a vacation to Galveston. She loved the ocean, and one night she just walked into the surf. Witnesses saw her go in. She left a note in her hotel room for me, saying she was sorry."

"Let me guess," LaRue said. "They never found her body?"

"No. She left the shop and its contents to me. Surprisingly, she'd already had a lucrative offer from someone to buy the place. They wanted it lock, stock, and barrel. I signed the paperwork and cleared out her personal effects. That's when I found it."

Owen fell silent. Gone were his normal theatrics, humor, and flamboyant gestures. The events of tonight had stripped him to his core. He seemed smaller somehow, and despite my dread about where all this was going, my heart went out to him.

"Found what?" I asked gently.

"A book filled with handwritten notes, newspaper articles, and other information on vampires, like how to become one, possible sightings, ways to kill them—that type of thing." Owen clenched his hands together on the table. They were shaking. "There was a newspaper clipping about Jad's death taped in the notebook and she'd written underneath it, 'is he really dead?' It was next to a list of dates and book titles. I believe the list showed the dates Jad visited the shop and the books he bought."

"Jad was going into that shop and buying books?" asked LaRue. "Why would he do that when the Van Helsing library was at his disposal?"

"Oh honey, he wasn't just there for the books," Owen said with a sympathetic glance my way. The writing was on the wall, but LaRue wasn't reading it, so he added another clue. "There were little red hearts drawn around the picture of Jad in the notebook."

You've heard the phrase, 'The lightbulb came on?' LaRue's lightbulb exploded. "That son of a bitch!" She bolted from her chair and circled the saloon, breathing deeply. Whether she was trying to calm down or keep from crying was anyone's guess. As the person who had been his wife, I felt strongly that I had first rights to anger and sadness about the fact that he'd had *another* mistress. Mistress number one, LaRue, obviously felt differently.

"I would kill the lying bastard if I could." She whirled on me. "What the hell were you doing kissing him tonight instead of staking his cheating heart?"

What the hell? Somehow the Voodoo Princess mistress had turned this around on me. I pushed to my feet, hands clenched, ready to let her have it.

"Ladies, ladies." Grace rose and placed herself between us. "Owen is telling us about his dearly not-so-departed sister, and the way in which he entered Laramie's life. There will be plenty of time to own up to each of your mistakes before the night has passed." She said the words with a friendly tone and a smile, but steel ran through both.

LaRue and I, knowing that she would not hesitate to grab us by the ears, plonked our butts back in our chairs and refocused on Owen with no further prompting.

Owen continued, "I never thought Ora Lee killed herself. I couldn't believe that after she fought so hard to live only a few years before, she would give up so easily when her business collapsed. And . . . this might sound strange, but being twins, we've always had a connection. Well, I never felt it break. When I saw her tonight, I wasn't really that surprised."

"I'm not buying it," Van said, scowling.

Owen nodded. "I agree that it doesn't make sense. Earlier, when Bunny asked about Ora Lee, I didn't remember seeing her or talking to her. But then the memories of tonight started coming back to me. And I don't think this is the first time I've seen her, either. I think she may have been the one who gave me the book with the newspaper clipping in it."

"See, love," Grace said, leaning over the table to get my attention. "This is why I sent your guests on their way earlier. Compellings don't always stick, especially when confronted with the truth of the matter soon after."

"How convenient for you to remember suddenly that

your vampire sister has been puppet mastering you," Van said, in a low, tight voice, as if Grace hadn't spoken. Then his restraint gave way, each word louder until he was shouting: "This doesn't absolve you from the way you've used Laramie!"

"Van!" I yelled. Our eyes met, and I held his gaze until he gained control of himself.

Then I turned to Owen. "Owen, were you aware of who I was when you responded to my ad for a web designer?"

Owen met my eyes, and when his gaze dropped it took my heart with it. I gulped Texas red from my oversized goblet and steeled myself.

"Yes," he whispered, and then continued in a stronger tone. "Yes. I had a Google alert set to your name, Jad's name, all of your family members, and The Madam after I found out that you had inherited her. When I received the alert for your advertisement, I figured it was divine intervention. I sent my resume to you the same day. Then I hacked into the ad and took it down."

"So that's why no one else ever applied?" I asked, stunned.

"That's why," Owen said. "But Laramie, I swear I never used you and I didn't have a clue about the supernatural thing. I just thought my sister must have gotten brainwashed by some married guy and they faked their deaths so they could run away together. No one was more surprised than I was the night you told me that vampires were real and you were turning into one."

He was referring to the night Van, LaRue and I had ambushed Marek at The Madam and performed a voodoo ceremony, trying to stop my change into a vampire. Owen had stumbled into the setup and I'd had to tell him everything.

My belief that Owen was my one true, friend disintegrated. He'd used me. His nosiness wasn't concern, after all. I flooded with shame, thinking about how easily I'd believed he liked me for who I was.

"You lied and manipulated me from the very beginning," I said. "How am I supposed to believe anything you say now?"

"I'm sure it's hard right now to believe it, but you know, deep down, that our friendship is real," Owen replied, his eyes earnest.

No, I didn't. Especially after everything else I'd learned tonight.

"If Jad and Ora Lee are working together, maybe they sent you here to spy on me," I said bitterly. Then I remembered that Star had told Van and me about that up on the widow's walk, when we were alone with her and Tiffany. "Jad venomed Ora Lee," I explained to the others.

Every head at the table nodded in response. Apparently, they'd already come to the same conclusion.

"Laramie, no," Owen protested. "I—"

"Jad changed Star, too," I interrupted. We had already told Grace, but the rest of the group needed to know.

LaRue looked stricken. "You don't know that! I bet Temple changed Star and sent her after us."

Now who was grasping at straws? Adam Temple was the Evil vampire who'd changed Jad in exchange for the True Cross. When Jad hadn't produced the relic, because he didn't have it, Temple had come after me. Temple fled after we bested him and I killed his mate, but he was still out there.

"No, LaRue," Van said gently. "Star told us that Jad made Ora Lee, Laramie, and her."

How many women had Jad been running around with? LaRue's snort let me know we were on the same wavelength.

"Before we go any further into this, Owen should leave," Van said stonily. "His motives are suspect, and he shouldn't know any more than he already does."

"Laramie, I swear, I was just trying to find out what happened to my sister." Owen's eyes were red. "But you and I became genuine friends along the way. I have never had to pretend or lie about how I feel for you. I've wanted to tell you everything, but the time just never seemed right. I value our friendship, and I want to be a part of this group."

When I made no reply he added, "But if you ask me to leave, I will."

Marek said, "Before you make your decision, I want to interject that while we found the connection between Owen's sister and Jad, we didn't find one between Owen and any others in the supernatural world." He turned to me. "Laramie, for what it is worth, I believe him. Owen has proven himself a trusted ally, and that is a rare thing in this world."

Those were strong words coming from Marek. His MO seemed to be to stay quiet and uninvolved unless he had to involve himself. I agreed with him in theory, but I was mad at Owen about something else, too.

"I can't believe that you had the gall to lecture me on my inability to have the tough conversations—"

"Laramie—" Owen began.

"I don't want to hear a single word from you," I said harshly, cutting him off. The dreaded pink mist was covering my vision. "You have been working alongside me for months. Insinuating yourself into my life. Taking a paycheck from me. Drinking my wine." I rose to my feet, still holding my wineglass. Its stem shattered in my grip and glass shards rained down on the table. Luckily, I had already drained it.

"Count, Laramie," Grace admonished.

"I don't feel like counting," I growled.

I tried to ignore the way Owen's face crumpled and looked to Van for support. He had pushed back from the table and appeared ready to defend himself. He was scared of me.

My anger washed away, and I sat heavily back in my chair. "Get out of my house," I said, staring at the shards of glass on the table.

"But Laramie—" Owen said.

"Get out! And don't come back."

"But . . . Dixie and I don't have anywhere else to go. I've already given my landlord notice and packed my stuff."

His words hurt me worse than Van's silver knife had. Didn't he understand how betrayed I felt? I had been looking forward to having company in the big, rambling house. But I couldn't trust him. Worse, I couldn't forgive him for making me lose my temper in front of Van. In that moment, I'd seen what Van really thought of me.

I looked up, and my eyes connected with Grace. She tried to throw me a lifeline when she nodded at me discreetly. Somehow I knew she was reminding me of Marek's words from earlier: *Keep your friends close and your enemies closer.*

I ignored the message and turned to Owen, looking him directly in the eye. "Then you should have told me the truth before it was forced out of you."

His face sagged. Without another word, he rose from his chair and slapped his leg. Dixie bolted out from under the table, gave a low growl at us, and then trotted on Owen's heels through the front door.

Bunny was horrified. "Laramie! You can't just let him go."

I shrugged, my shoulder twinging. I felt a million years old. "I can't live with someone who lies to me. Not again."

"Owen and Jad are nothing alike." She scraped back her chair and stood up, somehow still looking immaculate in her Playboy Bunny costume. "I may have just met Owen tonight, but he is a good person to the core and you know that."

"Bunny, he's been lying to her." Van reached out as if to lay his hand over mine, but seemed to think better of it and pulled back, putting it in his lap instead. "It's for the best."

Bunny walked to the front door of The Madam. Somewhere during the night she had lost her cape, and her cottontail quivered with indignation. She turned at the door and said, "I expected better of you." Her gaze pierced me first, then raked the table. "All of you."

20

DEAD TO ME

"And doesn't she have the right of it?" Grace said.

"Don't." I didn't want any lectures from Grace. Hadn't she just told me I needed to learn to deal with my problems? Well, I'd just dealt with the immediate problem by cutting Owen from the group. But part of me felt deeply sad. He'd looked so defeated, and Bunny was my almost-favorite Anderson. In the old days, she'd always taken my side against Van and Jad when they teased me. If she had raged at me, I could have taken it, but her disappointment hurt so much more.

And I couldn't stop worrying—where would Owen go now? Where would he and Dixie sleep? I steeled myself. I would not be a pushover. He had betrayed my trust and lied to me for over a year. I would not worry about him. I would focus on Van, and on making this thing between us work. He hadn't trusted me earlier tonight, and he'd been scared of me when I lost my temper, but he had reason. After all, I had killed him the night I changed. Under the circumstances, a little fear of me was probably healthy. And as Bunny had pointed out, Van brought all of his Van Helsing vampire baggage into this relationship. If I expected him to accept all of me, I must accept all of him, too.

The conversation had continued to flow around me, so I pushed all thoughts of Owen and Van away and tried to focus on what was being said.

"And why would it be that she has been compelling him, but not wiping him?" Grace asked Marek.

"Who?" I asked.

"Ora Lee," LaRue said between gritted teeth. She knew I hadn't been listening.

"She didn't understand what I was doing when I wiped Bill," Marek responded. "She has learned to compel, but not to wipe."

"There is sense to that," Grace replied thoughtfully. "It is easy to stumble onto the way of compelling, but someone has to teach you to wipe. Jad probably doesn't know the way of it either, since he had no maker to show him."

Wait, what was wiping? Were there different levels of compelling?

When I asked as much, Grace shook her head regretfully and muttered something about training. "Compelling is overlaying a thought or a memory," she explained. "You leave the original, but you cover it up with an inserted memory."

"Like you convinced the partygoers that the fight between Star, Ora Lee, and me was part of a show?" I asked.

She nodded. "Most of the lot took only a wee bit of compelling. But as you saw with Owen, the original memory can break through dead easy with the proper trigger. In serious cases—ones who are fierce excited or have experienced great trauma—you must first completely wipe a person's original memory and then insert the compelled memory."

"So then how do you get them to access the original memory if you need them to?" I asked, considering the attack on Gabrella. I wasn't sold on Tiffany's version of events.

"You can't," Marek said flatly. "It's gone."

Foreboding washed over me, but before I could ask which of my guests had had their memories erased tonight, LaRue pushed back from the table.

"I can't be a part of this any longer. All of you are so concerned about Laramie, but here is the truth of it. She is a vampire. Just like you two are vampires." She made a sweeping gesture at Grace and Marek. "And now two more of your type are on the loose: Star and Ora Lee. At least one of whom has no qualms about feasting on humans. And tonight, Grace and Marek showed us exactly how adept they are at making people forget how dangerous vampires are. I'm done dealing with blood suckers. I'm getting out of here before they compel me to believe this was all a bad dream, or worse, wipe my memory completely."

"LaRue," Van whispered as she turned to leave.

"No, Van, I'm leaving. I'll get an Uber."

She would have kept walking, but Van reached out and clasped her hand, stopping her. "Don't you want to know why Jad was here tonight?"

The hitch in LaRue's breathing proved that Van had hit the mark. She sat back down.

"Why *did* they come here tonight?" I asked. I had been wondering that myself. Plus, I would talk about anything right now, even my asshat ex, to push the image of Owen's sad face from my thoughts. Or to avoid acknowledging to myself that LaRue had just verbalized Van's own feelings about vampires. Which included me.

Van sighed. "My guess is that he still hasn't been able to locate the True Cross. I think he came back to The Bat Cave to pick up a resource book or books that he hopes might lead him to it. Ora Lee was probably acting as his lookout, outside. She must have seen Star come into the house and followed her, either to warn Jad or to keep Owen safe."

"You may have the right of it," Grace said, nodding in agreement.

Van, never one to give up an advantage, pressed on. "This proves my point. We have to go after the True Cross and find it before Jad or Temple do. Grace and Marek, you know where it is, or at least, you know more about it than we do. Jad has already created three new vampires. Those are just the ones we're aware of. He says he wants the cross to remove vampires from the earth, but if that were true, why does he keep creating them? We can't let him have it."

Marek shook his head. "Van, we can deal with Jad and Star without the True Cross. We've been dealing with rogue vampires for longer than you have," he added dryly. "But please admit the truth. Your motive isn't the safety of the True Cross. You only require it to change Laramie back into a human."

Van shouted, "Yes! Yes, I want it to change Laramie back. You didn't see her tonight. She nearly attacked an unconscious woman. When she smelled blood she couldn't control herself. She kissed Jad, for God's sake." His voice shook with anger. "Laramie isn't the person I fell in love with, and the True Cross is the only way to get her back."

If a heart could break, I was sure mine had. Van didn't love me. He couldn't—or wouldn't—accept me the way I was. A small whine came from under the table and a pittie head settled on my knee, reminding me what true love really felt like. I laid my trembling hand thankfully on Bo's head, letting her warmth soak into me.

Marek spoke, the weight of his conviction behind the words. "No. We will not look for the True Cross. We will not harm the many for the few. One life, one love, is not worth the price of a world at war."

Grace looked at me, pity in her eyes, and nodded. "We cannot, love."

Van focused on Marek. "Well, screw you, you selfish vampire bastard. Laramie and I will find it. We have the Van Helsing resources at our disposal. We won't stop."

"Van," I whispered. Then I continued in a stronger voice, "may I speak with you in the kitchen?"

"Laramie—"

"Van, please."

LaRue huffed out a breath, but Van nodded. I stood and moved at human speed across the saloon, trying to gather my thoughts and my words as we went.

We entered the kitchen and I stopped the motion of the swinging door behind us. We deserved privacy for this conversation. Van opened his mouth to speak, but I held up my hand to stop him.

"Van, do you really believe that even as a vampire, I would hide Jad in the Bat Cave and kiss him of my own free will?"

His eyes were tormented. "Laramie, you've been different since you changed. I just don't know."

"But I've hardly seen you since The Change. Where is this coming from?"

His nostrils flared. "Well, you drained me, for one thing."

Now we were at the heart of the matter.

"And I'm sorry about that. I have no excuse, but the fact that I feel really bad about it should count in my favor." That sounded weak, even to my ears.

"Laramie, I know you feel bad about it. And you regret kissing Jad. And I saw how you struggled to resist blood tonight. But feeling bad about your impulses doesn't mean you don't have them." He took me by the shoulders. "We'll find the True Cross on our own. We'll change you back and you won't want to drink blood or kiss your ex-husband. Problem solved." His hands fell to his sides. Was that distaste I saw on his face? Did he hate touching me that much?

Clearly, he still didn't believe me about Jad. He thought he was being magnanimous by sticking by me now that I was a vampire, until he could change me back to human.

But he wasn't. Not really. Believe me, I wanted to swoon into his arms, go find the True Cross, and live happily ever after. But I couldn't live my life, vampire or otherwise, with someone whose love was conditional. I ignored the little voice whispering that I'd had the same thoughts about myself earlier, when I'd nearly dropped to the floor to drink from Gabrella. Really, when it all boiled down, I was convinced I had done pretty well tonight. The blood had distracted me, but as Grace had pointed out, I hadn't bitten anyone.

I drew myself up. "No, Van. I'm okay with being a vampire. I would never have chosen this life for myself, but I'll be alright. I would rather live as a vampire than jeopardize the hiding place of the True Cross and unleash havoc on the world."

Van shook his head as if to clear it and opened his mouth to speak, but I took his hands in mine. I had to give it one more shot. "I didn't knowingly kiss Jad. You may not believe that, but I didn't. Yes, I struggled with blood tonight, but I resisted. At the core, I'm still the same Laramie as before, just with a few new challenges to overcome. Loving someone means accepting that person in all their parts. If you love me, you will believe me about Jad, and we can face the challenges being a vampire brings together."

I gazed at him, memorizing the blue eyes and lean face, lightly tanned against the white shirt of his vampire costume. He was far too handsome to make a believable Bela Lugosi. As the seconds ticked by without a rebuttal, I allowed myself to hope. Then he shook his head and eased his hands from mine. I followed him to the kitchen doorway and from there, watched him walk across the saloon. Relief shot through me when he stopped at The Madam's front door and turned to face me. I took a few steps in his direction, but when he didn't move toward me, I paused. He fished in his pocket and fiddled with something, then quietly placed his keys to The Madam on the hall table. Then, with LaRue behind him, Van walked through the front door and out of my life.

21

GONE

After they left, I looked around the saloon that only a few hours before had held so much promise and happiness. Grace, Marek, and I were alone, save for Bo. Now, taking in the open bottles of wine, the table of leftovers, and the dirty glasses and cups, I knew I couldn't deal with it tonight. The mess, both the physical and the emotional, would have to wait until tomorrow.

But it wasn't to be.

"Tomorrow we will teach you to wipe and compel," Marek told me. "Afterward, you must find Owen and wipe his memory of any traces of vampires or the supernatural."

I remembered how Owen's face had glowed earlier in the evening when he had proclaimed: "The Cabernet Cavalry rides again!" He had loved being a part of the group as much as I had. I knew I had to cut him out of our lives, but to erase the memories of our friendship and all we had been through?

"Couldn't you—"

"No," Grace said firmly, her features tight with anger. "Let this be a lesson in your training: It was your decision to remove him from your life. Now it is your duty to protect the rest of us from the knowledge he possesses."

I gave the vampires a slight nod, then turned my back on them. "See yourselves out," I said as I refilled my wineglass. I shook the bottle to make sure I got every drop out of it. With Bo on my heels, I grabbed another open bottle on the way to the back staircase, then trudged up the three flights to my apartment.

Utterly exhausted, I let myself into my rooms on The Madam's third floor. Despite now being considered a creature of the night, I rigorously kept a daytime schedule. I wanted nothing more than to sleep in my own bed.

It wasn't until I saw the boys zonked out together on the couch that I remembered Daisy was asleep in my bedroom. I didn't have it in me to trudge downstairs to one of the guest rooms. It would be a night on the floor for me.

I eased open the door to my turret bedroom and crossed the small space to retrieve an extra blanket from a wardrobe that hugged one wall. When its ancient hinges screeched I froze, but there was no movement from the bed. So I tiptoed over to ease one of my pillows free.

I needn't have bothered. The bed was empty.

I turned on the lights and surveyed the room. When my eyes landed on the piece of paper on my bedside table, my heart sank, and I sat down heavily on the bed. Bo jumped up to join me.

I scanned the words and then read them more carefully. I couldn't make sense of the note Daisy had left.

Bo nudged me with her head. I got under the covers and after a low whine, she snuggled against me. I thought of my brother's young sons asleep on my couch, left behind by their mother, and of the call I would have to make to Monty tomorrow.

For the first time in the two weeks since I'd become a vampire, I cried.

EPILOGUE: SOMETHING WICKED THAT WAY GOES

The Safe House
Somewhere in Dallas

"What the hell happened in there?" Ora Lee demanded when she joined him at their meetup location.

"A minor glitch, that's all," Jad soothed, attempting to kiss her, not wanting to show her how worried he'd been.

"Get off me," she ordered, pushing him away. "You kissed Laramie."

"Now darling, calm down."

Her reaction was as immediate as if he had tossed gasoline on her. "Calm down? While I chased that psycho vampire Star through the house, you were busy making out with your wife. Then I had to fight the crazy bitch to keep her from hurting said wife, plus her friends and family, because you ran out the back door. And Owen," her voice hitched, "nearly died because of me. I had to compel him to forget about me. Again."

"Oh sweetheart, I'm sorry. You've been through the ringer tonight, haven't you?"

At that, she finally let him pull her into his arms.

"But I got it," he murmured into her hair. "And I couldn't chance them seeing it. We agreed that the mission would come first."

She raised her head to look at him, her copper-colored eyes gleaming in the dark. "Yes, but I don't see what the big deal is. They've had it the whole time."

He nodded. "Yeah. They don't realize how important it is. I only figured it out after I traced Grace and Marek's past. If those two saw me with it, they would know where we're looking for the True Cross."

"I understand, but . . . I think if we went to Grace and Marek and came clean, we could all look together," Ora Lee said.

He shook his head. "That's the plan, but they aren't ready yet. If it was up to Van and Laramie, maybe, but Grace and Marek won't work with us. If they have any idea how close we are, they'll move it."

"You're really convinced they know where it's at?"

"They've kept it safe for centuries. You don't quit a job like that," Jad replied grimly.

"What do we do now?"

"We have to take care of Star before we can continue looking for the cross. She's gotten too good at tracking us." His grip on her tightened. "This is the last time she ambushes us. From now on, we become the hunters."

ENJOYED THE STORY?

Thank you for reading *The Blood Will Tell*. If you enjoyed Laramie's party, please consider leaving a review where you bought the book. I appreciate your help in spreading the word, and reviews make a tremendous difference in helping new readers find the series.

Join my newsletter, **The Night Club**, at jckeough.com for notifications of giveaways and new releases, along with personal updates from behind the scenes of my books. To sweeten the cauldron, you will receive my short story "Dinner with the Delaneys" for free.

ALSO BY J.C. KEOUGH

THE LARAMIE HARPER CHRONICLES

Dying in Dallas

The Blood Will Tell

Whining in Wolf Land - Coming in 2021

Do you want to read a short story about Star?

Join my newsletter, **The Night Club** at **JCKeough.com**, to receive the short story "Dinner with the Delaneys" and to be notified when *Whining in Wolf Land*, the 3rd book in the LARAMIE HARPER CHRONICLES is released.

ABOUT THE AUTHOR

J.C. Keough is the creator of the LARAMIE HARPER CHRONICLES. Jamie is working on the third book in the series and the first book in a new series named THE TEXAS TENDER MYSTERIES. The Tender Mysteries will combine beer, boats, murders, and ghosts.

Jamie lives in a small town on the Southwest coast of Ireland with her husband and their two fur babies.

You can find out more at www.jckeough.com

AUTHOR'S NOTE

Thank you for reading *The Blood Will Tell*. I knew, before I ever finished *Dying in Dallas*, that I had to write a Halloween story for Laramie. I planned a quick, short story to update readers on what happened immediately after her change into a vampire.

But, in the usual way of my writing, it got longer and longer, and I ended up with a novella. For those of you unfamiliar with a novella (I had never even heard the term until I started writing), it is longer than a short story, but shorter than a full-length novel. At just under 30,000 words, *The Blood Will Tell* is just over a fourth of the length of *Dying in Dallas*. That is also why I have it listed as book 1.5 in the series.

As I move forward with THE LARAMIE HARPER CHRONICLES, I will be writing the books in a novel, novella, novel, release format. The novels will be longer books with a murder mystery and furthering the search for the True Cross. The novellas will focus on the characters and their stories at The Whine Barrel.

Without giving too much away, book 3, *Whining in Wolf Land*, will focus on finding Laramie's sister-in-law, Daisy, and Grace and Laramie's search for the True Cross in Ireland.

I hope you will join the Cabernet Cavalry on that adventure.

www.ingramcontent.com/pod-product-compliance
Lightning Source LLC
LaVergne TN
LVHW091558060526
838200LV00036B/888